7TH FLOOR
Museum Offices

6TH FLOOR
Collection Storage
Not open to the public

**3RD-FLOOR
GALLERIES**

Really Big Urns
Gallery of Painted Girls
Beetles, Buttons, Crowns
Japanese Ceremonial Dress
Gallery of Colonial Expansion
Re-created Edwardian Parlor
17th-Century Ceramics
Life in Mongolia
Carnival Masks
Thimbles

2ND-FLOOR GALLERIES

Dresses
Oriental Tapestries
Alchemy: The Exhibition
Refectory, Farming Equipment
Dollhouses and Dolls
Women in the 19th Century
Gallery of Wolves
Stuffed Elephants
Re-created 19th-Century Street

OPHELIA

AND THE

MARVELOUS

BOY

Ophelia and the Marvelous Boy

✦

KAREN FOXLEE

ALFRED A. KNOPF
NEW YORK

THIS IS A BORZOI BOOK PUBLISHED BY ALFRED A. KNOPF

Visit us on the Web! randomhouse.com/kids

Educators and librarians, for a variety of teaching tools, visit us at RHTeachersLibrarians.com

Library of Congress Cataloging-in-Publication Data
Foxlee, Karen.
Ophelia and the marvelous boy / Karen Foxlee. — First edition.
p. cm.
Summary: Ophelia, a timid eleven-year-old girl grieving her mother, suspends her disbelief in things non-scientific when a boy locked in the museum where her father is working asks her to help him complete an age-old mission.
ISBN 978-0-385-75354-8 (trade) — ISBN 978-0-385-75355-5 (lib. bdg.) — ISBN 978-0-385-75357-9 (ebook)
[1. Magic—Fiction. 2. Prisoners—Fiction. 3. Museums—Fiction. 4. Heroes—Fiction. 5. Wizards—Fiction. 6. Kings, queens, rulers, etc.—Fiction.] I. Title.
PZ7.F841223Oph 2014
[Fic]—dc23
2013012236

The text of this book is set in 12-point Bell MT.

Printed in the United States of America
January 2014
10 9 8 7 6 5 4 3 2 1

First Edition

For my sister, Sonia

THE NORTH WIND DOTH BLOW
AND WE SHALL HAVE SNOW

In the end the Queen was nothing like she was in the stories the Marvelous Boy had been told, first as a child beside the hearth and later by the wizards. There were no claws. No sharp teeth. She was young. Her pale hair dripped over her shoulders. She opened her blue eyes wide and smiled sweetly at the King.

"I do not like him, my darling," she said, not once raising her voice. "I do not like him one little bit."

"B-b-but he is my Marvelous Boy," stammered the King. He hated to disappoint her; they were only newly wed.

"That is the problem exactly," she said. "They tell me he does not age. That he has been here ten years yet looks just as he did when he arrived. That his hair has not grown, nor his body. It makes me uneasy. I cannot sleep peacefully while he is free to roam. And this story they tell me, of the sword he carries. How can I feel safe when I hear such a thing?"

1

"Now, now," said the King. "For many years, he has been my faithful companion."

"I should like him locked away," she said.

"Locked away?"

"We shall lock him away. He shall be locked in a room and allowed out only to be exhibited. He shall be displayed beside all my other precious things; he is a curiosity. I will feel safer."

"I don't know," said the King. "He is a good boy; he means no harm."

The new Queen narrowed her eyes at him.

The snow had already begun by then, and now it did not end. It covered the palace grounds, the once-green gardens, the Herald Tree. It blanketed the hills and the fields. It covered houses. Whole villages simply disappeared. The lakes froze over, and then the sea. Children's faces grew thin and gray. Old ladies keeled over and froze in the streets.

When the room was ready, the Marvelous Boy was led along the great corridors. In the palace there were hundreds of rooms and hundreds of staircases and hundreds of glass cabinets. Displayed there were her jewels and her other still trophies: snow lions and leopards, white elephants, snowy owls—a whole room of them, frozen in time, their wings pinned open on the mounting boards.

There were great mosaic floors depicting the wedding pageant of the King and Queen and wintry worlds and sea monsters eating boatloads of people.

"Whatever made you think of that?" asked the King about the sea monsters.

"It was a story I once heard," said the Queen, "and I enjoyed it so."

She really was very cruel.

The boy did not struggle as he was led to his room. He had struggled already. Three times since the wedding he had tried to run from the city, and three times he had been returned.

Around the door there had been painted a mural of his marvelous journey. In the mural the boy stood with his magical sword raised, but at the door his sword was taken from him and handed to the King. His satchel too, which contained the instructions and his compass. The boy looked to the King, but the King would not return his gaze. Inside his room there was nothing but a bed and chair and one window, high up. The Queen smiled and looked very pleased. She fingered the key on the chain at her throat.

"You have failed in everything you set out to do," she said when they were alone, just the Marvelous Boy and her. "I do not know why the wizards chose you, such a poor, sorry thing. Why did they think you could defeat me?" She did not pause for his answer. "And this charm that is bestowed on you so that I cannot harm you—it is nothing but an irritation. When the charm has worn off, I will run you through with my sword. What are years to me? I shall build a clock to count the seconds and minutes and days and years, and when they are passed, its chimes will sound, yes, and I will harm you greatly."

She said it very pleasantly, as though she were talking about marshmallows or afternoon tea.

"I will find the sword," the boy whispered. "And the one who will wield it."

"It will be destroyed," said the Queen, "melted down, chopped into a thousand pieces."

"We will find a way to defeat you," said the boy.

Which made the Queen very amused, so that she laughed quite merrily. Then she left him there, closed his door, and turned the key.

· PART ONE ·

1

*In which Ophelia Jane Worthington-Whittard
discovers a boy in a locked room and
is consequently asked to save the world*

———◆———

Ophelia did not consider herself brave. She wasn't like Lucy Coutts, the head girl in her grade, who once rescued a baby in a runaway stroller and was on the front page of all the papers. Lucy Coutts had heavy brown hair and pink cheeks, and she called Ophelia *Scrap*, which made everyone laugh, even Ophelia, to show she didn't mind.

Ophelia didn't consider herself brave, but she was very curious.

She was exactly the kind of girl who couldn't walk past a golden keyhole without looking inside.

The keyhole was in a foreign city where it always snowed. It was on the third floor of the museum, in the 303rd room. Ophelia wasn't at all sure how she got there, only that she let her feet take her wherever they wanted to go.

Her father had taken a job at the museum. He had become,

at the eleventh hour, the curator of *Battle: The Greatest Exhibition of Swords in the History of the World.* The previous curator had left without warning. In three days, Ophelia's father was to prepare hundreds of swords to be exhibited on Christmas Eve.

He also hoped that a week in a foreign city would be just the medicine for his daughters. They could explore and ice-skate while he worked. And they would have a white Christmas away from their home, which had grown so quiet.

He was very busy, though, far too busy to spend much time with them. He told Ophelia she must stay close to her older sister, Alice. But Alice was not interested in seeing any of the attractions. She wanted to go nowhere and do nothing. She wanted to sit all day with her headphones, playing gloomy music and thinking gloomy thoughts. She'd been like that ever since their mother died, which was exactly three months, seven days, and nine hours ago.

"I'll take you ice-skating later," Alice said, but in a very halfhearted way.

So, all morning Ophelia had walked alone. She had been upstairs and down. She had climbed in and out of elevators that rattled and creaked between the floors. There were grand galleries filled with priceless treasures and glittering halls filled with dazzling relics. There were precious paintings by the old masters and glorious statues and huge urns, and the ceilings danced with painted angels. Ophelia tried, as hard as she could, to be interested in all these things.

She leaned her head to one side and nodded approvingly.

She looked up interesting facts in the rather useless guide.

She tried to stifle all her yawns.

But fortunately, these glimmering places also led to murky corridors. And these murky corridors also led to dimly lit rooms. And these rooms contained smaller, stranger collections. And it was these places that made Ophelia's heart beat faster.

She found a lonely room filled with teaspoons.

Which led to a room containing only telephones.

Which led to a shadowy arcade of mirrors.

She passed through an exhibition of stuffed and preserved elephants. She tiptoed through a quiet pavilion filled with the threadbare taxidermied bodies of wolves. She squeezed through the crowd in the *Gallery of Time* and saw the famous Wintertide Clock. It ticked so loudly that people had to stick their fingers in their ears. She ran down a long, dim hallway filled with melancholy paintings of girls.

It was very cold. Windows were left open to stinging sparks of sleet and snow. The wind whistled and moaned through the galleries and down the stairwells. It made the cobwebs on the chandeliers dance.

Even with a map it was a very confusing place. Signs pointed in the wrong directions, and no one bothered about fixing them. The sign for *Porcelains 1700–1850 AD* led to *Costumes and Culture of the Renaissance*. The sign for *Costumes and Culture of the Renaissance* led to *Bronze Age Artifacts*. The sign for *Bronze Age Artifacts* led to an imposing red, locked door.

There was no point in asking the guards. The guards sat in corners and knitted or dozed. Sometimes, they snarled and yelled like banshees for no good reason, and other times, they let children climb on the glass cabinets, using the brass handles for footholds. Sometimes, they came rushing at people who just happened to stand too long in one place, and other times, they smiled huge toothless smiles and offered old fruit from their large black handbags.

The museum in the city where it always snowed was the type of place where a person could very easily get lost. Miss Kaminski, the museum curator, had said so herself. Miss Kaminski was dazzlingly beautiful. Her blond hair was tied in an elegant chignon, and she was surrounded by a cloud of heavenly perfume. She had smiled at Ophelia and Alice before placing a perfectly manicured hand on their father's arm.

"It is advisable that they do not wander alone," Miss Kaminski said. "The museum is very big, and several girls have become lost and never been found."

But Ophelia didn't feel afraid. It was much better on her own. It was a relief to be out of the workroom, where her father had begun work as soon as they arrived in the city. He was unpacking swords and polishing swords and cataloging swords endlessly. Her father knew everything there was to know about swords. His card read:

MALCOLM WHITTARD

LEADING INTERNATIONAL EXPERT ON SWORDS

"I have a very tight deadline, Ophelia. Christmas Eve!" he said whenever Ophelia tried to talk to him. "I'm sure there are more than enough things here to keep you and Alice occupied."

If ever you have the chance to visit this museum, the keyhole to room 303 is quite close to a much-celebrated sea monster mosaic floor. It is marked on the maps by an octopus symbol. That first morning, Ophelia spent some time walking on the mosaic waves and the mosaic foam. She traveled the length of all eight glittering tentacles, observed the people falling back from the monster's mouth. She bent over and looked directly into its eye.

It was the sort of thing her mother would have loved. Ophelia Jane Worthington-Whittard wished more than anything that her mother were alive.

Near the sea monster mosaic floor, she noticed a gallery with a red rope hung across its entrance. Ophelia slipped under the rope and went inside. It was a small exhibition of broken stone angels. There was no guard in the room, so she touched some wings, even though she knew she shouldn't have. It was very quiet and very still. All she could hear was her own footsteps and her own breathing. It had a peculiar, empty smell. No one had been that way for a very long time.

In the corner of the room there was a very normal-looking gray door. Above the door were the small silver numbers 302. Ophelia opened it.

The room behind the ordinary gray door was also almost normal. The floor was checkerboard. The tall windows, with tatty velvet curtains pulled back, gave a view of the city. The sky was also gray.

The room would have also been ordinary if it wasn't for the little stage at its end and the faded mural of mountains and a blue sea and a boy with a sword. Above this scene, painted in golden letters, cracked and peeling, stretching in an arch, were the words:

THE MARVELOUS BOY

There was a small door. It was hidden among the peaked blue waves with their little whitecaps, and in the small door there was a golden keyhole.

Ophelia crossed the checkerboard floor and climbed one step up onto the stage and walked across the floorboards. She knelt down to the keyhole and pressed her eye against it to see inside.

She did it without thinking.

It was the type of girl she was.

She did not expect anything unusual.

She did not expect to be looking straight into a large blue-green eye.

"Hello," said the owner of the eye, a boy's voice. "I come in friendship and mean you no harm."

Ophelia was on her bottom, crawling backward away from the door. Her heart was lurching and leaping inside her chest. She felt for her puffer in her blue velvet coat pocket and gave herself a squirt.

"Who are you?" she said, or at least tried; her words came out squeaky.

"I don't have a name," said the voice. "It was taken from me by a protectorate of wizards from the east, west, and middle to keep me safe."

"But I don't believe in wizards," Ophelia said.

"Come closer," said the voice.

Anyone would say, *"Don't go closer."* Ophelia wasn't stupid. In fact, she belonged to the Children's Science Society of Greater London, which met on Tuesday nights. Of course she wouldn't go closer. It was only common sense.

Ophelia knelt, staring at the mural. The beautiful mountain range, the turquoise sea, the boy with the solemn expression and his sword raised. She pulled down hard on her braids, because that sometimes made her feel better.

"Why can't you come out?" Ophelia asked.

"I'm locked in."

"A prisoner?"

"Yes," said the voice.

Ophelia could have walked away. She could have picked herself up and walked backward from the room. She could have followed her feet all the way past the stone angels and across the sea monster mosaic. She could have run down the long hallway of painted girls and squeezed through the crowd in the *Gallery of Time*. She could have raced down, down, down the damp, creaking stairs to her father, cataloging and classifying swords. When Mr. Whittard asked her what she'd been doing, she could have said, "Absolutely nothing. It's very boring here."

But she didn't. She walked on her hands and knees slowly toward the keyhole.

"What do you want?" she asked.

The blue-green eye was surrounded by dark lashes. When the owner of the eye leaned back, she could see it was a boy. He had a pleasant enough face. He wiped his bangs out of his eyes. When he smiled, a dimple appeared in his right cheek.

"I need your help," the boy said, "to save the world."

Ophelia wasn't expecting that. It made her cross.

"I'm so glad you came, even if you are very late," he continued. "I've had only Mr. Pushkinova to speak to and I haven't been allowed out for ages now that the ending is near."

"Who's keeping you in there?" Ophelia asked.

"I am a prisoner of Her Majesty, the Snow Queen," said the boy.

"But I don't believe in Snow Queens."

"Do you believe in magical swords?"

"Well . . . ," said Ophelia. She didn't want to sound impolite.

"Great magical owls? Misery birds?"

"Who?"

"What about ghosts?" asked the boy, leaning forward again.

She thought awhile. The smile in the large blue-green eye faltered; the lid closed momentarily.

"Ghosts?" the boy asked again.

Ophelia chewed her fingernail. "I might believe," she said, "in the possibility of ghosts, but I'm not sure. I need to research the evidence more."

"What *do* you believe in?" asked the boy.

She didn't like his tone. "I believe in lots of things," Ophelia said, trying to sound very certain. "There was a big bang; all the stars are still traveling apart right now. The moon is a certain distance from us, but sometimes it comes closer and sometimes farther—that's how it pushes the sea. Everything in the whole world can be classified scientifically. For instance, I am from the kingdom Animalia, phylum Chordata, class Mammalia, order Primates, family Hominidae, genus *Homo*, species *Homo sapiens*. I only eat class Pisces and only if they're called sardines. I don't believe in unicorns or dragons or anything magical, really."

She took her mouth away from the keyhole and pressed her eye there.

"Well, they only give me porridge to eat," said the boy, "and everyone knows unicorns and dragons aren't real. But you may believe in ghosts?"

"Maybe," she said.

"Good, I must tell you many things," he said. "If you choose to help me, you must find the key to this door. We need to find my sword, which is magical, and the One Other, who will know how to wield it. On the Wintertide Clock there is a number in the little window at the very bottom of the face, just below the door of chimes, that will tell us how much time we have."

Ophelia bit her bottom lip.

"I told my father I'd only be gone a little while," she said.

"Please, Ophelia," said the boy.

Of course she couldn't save the world. She was only eleven years old and rather small for her age, and also she had knock-knees. Dr. Singh told her mother she would probably grow out of them, especially if she wore medical shoes, but that wasn't the point. She had very bad asthma as well, made worse by cold weather and running and bad scares. Ophelia thought this should have all been proof that she couldn't possibly help. She leaned away from the keyhole.

Everything was meant to be simple. Mr. Whittard was to work, and Alice and Ophelia were to ice-skate. They'd go to the rink in the city square beneath the giant Christmas tree. A foreign city was meant to take their minds off terrible things. Ice-skating would help them forget some of their sadness. Now here was a boy asking her to do impossible things. He was making everything unsimple.

"After you have been to the Wintertide Clock, you must find the elevator in the dinosaur hall," said the boy. "That will take you to the seventh floor. You will need to take the left corridor. The right corridor leads to the Queen's chamber. The left corridor is where the misery birds are kept—you must be careful not to wake them. At the very end of the corridor, there will be a small white cupboard with a small white drawer. You must bring the key that is in that drawer to me."

He's full of orders, thought Ophelia. Check the clock, take this elevator here, get that key there.

"Why were you chosen by a protectorate of wizards?" she asked. The best way to get to the bottom of things was with questions. "And how can someone take your name from you? I don't think that's really possible."

The boy sighed. The sigh of someone who is in a hurry but who knows he has to stop and go back to the very beginning to get anywhere.

"Sit closer," he said. "And I'll tell you." Through the keyhole, the boy said:

* * *

You might think things fade with time. Memories, I mean. But they don't. They grow stronger. I can still see the river beside the city, where I played with Julius and Rohan and Fred. We skipped stones there and built rafts and sailed all the way to the weir.

When I was chosen, people didn't understand. They said, "Why, him—he's nothing but an ordinary boy." But the wizards, they were never ones to listen to such talk. They always know exactly what they are doing because they learn it from standing very still and thinking for hours.

The wizards had asked for every boy child, aged twelve, to be brought to the town square.

"There is a boy child who shall undertake a treacherous journey to deliver a magical sword to the One Other so that the Snow Queen may be defeated," the Great Wizard said in his calm, low voice.

"We have dreamt him," the wizards said together. "We have seen him in our visions."

My mother, on hearing this, was not impressed at all. "I think we'll go fishing instead," she said.

All day we went about the forest and caught spangled trout, a whole bucketful, and even when I was tired, she wouldn't go home. Of course, I know now it was because she sensed the boy to be chosen was me.

While we were gone, the boys lined up in the square. There were some girls too, dressed as boys, because some mothers desire their children to do great things and thought there might be some benefits that came with the role. When my mother and I came home, it was well after dark and she thought we were safe. But there was the Great Wizard sitting at our small kitchen table, waiting.

"He is the one," he said.

"How do you know?" said my mother, who wasn't shy of a fight.

You might think wizards are always casting spells and stirring cauldrons and changing tin into gold, and it's true that sometimes they do, but mostly they are known for their trances and their thinking and their staring ahead until the future comes swimming into view. They can see the future in puddles and in dewdrops and sometimes even in shiny spoons.

"Because it has been seen," sighed the wizard. "And because he is so good. The Snow Queen will desire him, and he will lead her away from here to the other realm. And once there he will destroy her."

Good.

Not brave or strong or super.

These were the traits the town folk thought the decision should have been based upon. But it was because I was *good.* Well, they didn't like that. And no amount of explaining settled them down for some time.

"The Snow Queen likes more than anything else to destroy good things," the wizards explained. "She likes good things to become bad things, bad things to become sad things, sad things to become eternally frozen things."

But the town folk soon forgot. It was still summer, you see, and the threat of an invasion from the north seemed impossible. The wheat was waving golden in the fields and the roses were as big as dinner plates.

"You're just an ordinary boy," my mother muttered as she got me ready for my first day of education in the wizard house. "You don't know the first thing about swords and journeys. And you're bone lazy and always forgetting things."

Yet she deposited me at the door of the wizard house and tried not to cry. She brushed down my hair with her hands, and told me to be good and listen to what was being taught.

They took my name. That was the first thing they did. They took it from me with a spell, and one of the young wizard apprentices grabbed it and placed it in a scruffy velvet box.

Now, you might say this is impossible, but only because you have never had your name taken. The King himself could not believe it when I arrived here. He told me many times that all I had to do was sit down in a quiet place and think hard about it. But no amount of thinking could get my name back. In my mind there was nothing but a clean space, like a freshly painted wall. And it was the same for everyone else who knew me—my mother, for instance, when she came to collect me in the afternoon. She went to say my name and stopped, and tears filled up her eyes.

And you might think a name is just a name, nothing but a word, but that is not the case. Your name is tacked to you. Where it has joined you, it has seeped into your skin and into your essence and into your soul. So when they plucked my name from me with their spell, it was as heavy as a rock in their hands but as invisible as the wind, and it wasn't just the memory of my name, but me myself. A tiny part of me that they took and stored away.

It was hoped that if they kept that part of me when I crossed to the other world, then they would be able to help me back again. But they weren't very sure. No one had been that way for a long time.

When I realized my name was gone, I was angry as a wild boar. I stamped around in the upstairs school, which was just a bare room with a wooden floor and no seat and no table. I was made to stand there for hours and hours. I was made to listen to their lessons, which were all about being polite and standing still and listening to trees and about nothing magical at all. That first day I banged on the walls. I shouted, "Give me my name back!"

The Great Wizard himself came and told me to stop making a racket. Wizards don't much like noise, you see. Regarding the name, the Great Wizard said in his slow, calm voice, "Well, you'll get used to it in time, and it is only for your own good. If the protectorate keeps your name, it will allow you to return one day through the meridian, which is the point of no return between that world and this. Or at least that is what we hope."

Which didn't make me feel very confident.

All that summer I had to go to them each day, and they taught me what they could. They taught me how I must always tell the truth and always stop to help those who needed help, and something about magical owls, but I missed that part because I wasn't listening. I had to repeat again and again, "I am a boy chosen by a protectorate of wizards from the east, west, and middle to deliver this sword so that the Snow Queen may be defeated." My voice grew hoarse from saying that. And they taught me that, in the other world, I would find a kind and just ruler.

And I asked them, "Well, do you know his or her name?" and they just stared at me patiently.

But I got used to those wizards, who really are very kind. If you have heard it said that wizards eat nothing but biscuits, then you have heard the truth. The biscuits at the wizard house were made by Petal, who was not tall and thin like the others, but short and round. And also she was a woman and also seemingly a wizard, which made even less sense to me.

On that first day they let me down from the schoolroom and deposited me in the kitchen, where Petal was kneading dough. She was sitting in a slant of sunlight from the large kitchen windows, her red hair aflame, her large arms working the dough. She banged the dough with her fist and picked it up and slammed it on the table so that clouds of flour rose and settled in showers over her. She smiled at me.

"I'm going to make biscuits," she said.

I didn't answer, but scowled.

Petal had a broad, calm face browned by the sun and very large, pleasantly freckled hands. "Are you terribly sad about your name?" she asked.

"Well, wouldn't you be?" I replied.

"I would. It's true. I would. But one day it will be yours again."

"But I want it back now. It was mine, and stealing is wrong."

"Indeed," said Petal. "Indeed." She took a small piece of dough and roughly made it into the shape of a little man. "Here, watch this." She took the little man and cupped him near her mouth and breathed a tiny soul into him. She put him on the table, and he stood up and danced its length, spinning and turning and doing cartwheels.

It was the first piece of magic that I had seen in the house, and it made me laugh.

"Can you do it again?" I asked.

"I could," she said. "But then I would have to lie down for the rest of the day, and there is work to be done."

The wizards smell like the earth and mushrooms. The smell of them stays in the room for hours after they've gone. Yes, I got used to those wizards in a way.

All the while that summer, everyone was waiting for her. The Snow Queen, I mean. At first it seemed too difficult to believe in such a thing. Then the first of the refugees appeared from the north, skinny and starving, children, mainly, who had managed to escape her. They said she had teeth like razors and hair like a blizzard and she carried a sword called the Great Sorrow.

When the wizards heard that, they said, "It is as we have seen."

Which didn't make the town folk feel confident at all. The

forges worked day and night, making weapons. Everyone looked to the horizon. People were spooked by certain clouds coming over the grasslands and swamps. They packed up their belongings, ready to take flight, then unpacked them again when they realized they were nothing but ordinary clouds on ordinary days.

They complained to the wizards. Why would they spend such time bothering with a boy? Why could they not fight the Snow Queen with their magic? The wizards didn't say much to that. They took me into the forest. They taught me which plants to eat and which not to. They taught me how to shoot with a bow and arrow. I quite enjoyed that until I had to kill a rabbit, which was horrible. They showed me how to lay my hands on the Herald Tree, which was a very strange education.

"You keep talking about a sword, yet I haven't seen one," I said in the wizard house. "Is it all make-believe?"

They smiled serenely at that.

"I mean, none of it makes sense," I said. "This One Other, for instance, who is that? Shouldn't you give me some details? Like what he looks like?"

They smiled even more serenely, and it was a good thing they hadn't given me the sword yet.

Each night I went home, and my mother met me at the door and examined me to see if I'd changed at all. She had been very annoyed about my name in the beginning but had gotten used to it. *My boy* was what she had taken to calling me, and it was quite comforting.

"What did you learn, then?" she asked me each day.

All I could do was shrug.

The morning I left the kingdom, I woke with the wizards standing above me, in our very own little house, without even having knocked. For three days the air had cooled, though it was still summer. The fruit had browned and fallen from the trees. Everywhere people were bundling their daughters onto horses and their grandmothers into wagons, and whole processions of people were leaving the city. The river was covered in a lacework of ice.

That morning my mother didn't say much but held my face between her hands.

"I don't want to go," I said.

"Hush now. It's you that's been chosen and there's nothing we can do about it," she said.

"Will I see you again?"

How she cried at that.

"Please," I said. "Tell me I'll see you again."

And she said, "Yes, yes, yes, my boy, of course you will."

Petal had made me some biscuit men, and my mother placed some bread and cheese inside my satchel. The wizards gave me the compass, which they told me must always point south.

"But I don't know what to do," I said. "You haven't taught me properly."

It was true—all their months of teaching me and I still couldn't make sense of it.

For instance, how was I meant to know who this One Other was? Couldn't they give me some sort of clue? But I dared not ask that again.

"Can't you write it down for me?" I said. "I mean, everything I'm meant to do, just in case I forget?"

So the Great Wizard wrote on a piece of paper very patiently, folded it three times, and placed it in with the biscuits. There were a bow and a quiver with just one arrow.

I said, "Is that enough?"

And they said, "It is all you will need."

Then they brought the sword, which I hadn't seen before and which was very heavy and very plain and not at all magical-looking. They tied it to my waist.

"We, the protectorate of wizards from the east, west, and middle, have made this sword so that the Snow Queen may be defeated," they said.

They put a spell on me. They lay their hands on me, all five of them. You see, they coated me in it, this spell. It was a dripping ointment–smelling one, and they said I should not get wet or the whole lot would come off.

"It will cover your scent, which the Queen will know," they said, "and hide you from her wolves and her owls."

After that I wasn't sure what I should do.

"Now, my boy," said the Great Wizard, "you should begin to run."

"I see," said Ophelia. It was all she could think to say. She thought she'd been very patient listening.

"You do?" said the boy behind the door.

"I really have to get back to my sister. We might go ice-skating, you see. I'll try and come back later," she said.

"Thank you, Ophelia," he said, although she could hear the disappointment in his voice.

She had the words *I'm sorry* on the tip of her tongue, but she didn't say them. She stood up, chewing her fingernail, walked across the checkerboard floor, and tried not to think of the blue-green eyes watching her. She tried not to think about how the boy knew her name. He'd said it twice, and she hadn't told him it. Not once. She tried not to think of anything. She could not help the boy because she didn't believe in him.

There, she'd thought it.

She didn't believe in wizards or boys with no names. These things could not be classified. These things could not be pigeonholed. These things made her feel terrible. She plunged her hands into her coat pockets to keep them warm. She walked through the gallery of broken stone angels, across the celebrated sea monster mosaic, upstairs and downstairs.

In her left pocket there was a map of the museum, and in her right pocket there was her puffer. There was also a small hole. She stuck her finger through the hole because for some reason, lately, that made her feel a little calmer.

If her mother had been alive, Ophelia would have told her about the hole. But she was not. Ophelia looked at her watch. Her mother had been gone exactly three months, seven days, and fourteen hours.

If Ophelia had shown her pocket to her mother, who was not practical at all, she would have sighed.

"Surely we have a needle and thread somewhere here," her mother would have said, and taken Ophelia from room to room in their house, looking in drawers and boxes. She might have found some twine or even some glue. She might have used her stapler; she'd done that once with the hem of Ophelia's school uniform. The stapler lived on her writing desk, right beside the vampire-teeth paperweight.

Ophelia stuck her finger through the hole. She felt it tear a little more. She was nothing like her mother, she thought. Her mother had believed in almost everything. Her mother had believed in vampires with satin cloaks and shape-shifters that slid through keyholes. She believed in the ghosts of children who terrorized schools and strange creatures who sucked the thoughts from their victims' brains. She loved crumbling castles and dark towers and secret doors.

Her mother wrote about these things. She wrote about these things all morning in her study. Her stories were sent away in bundles of paper tied up with string and returned as the books that lined the sitting room. Dark books. Thick books. Books with her name, Susan Worthington, emblazoned on the front in blood-red letters that glimmered in the dark.

Ophelia walked down the long gallery that contained the paintings of bored-looking girls in party dresses. She squeezed through the crowd in the *Gallery of Time*. She didn't bother at all to look for the little window in the clock that the boy had asked after.

She went through the pavilion of wolves and the exhibition of elephants. She stamped through the arcade of mirrors, the room filled with telephones, the gallery of teaspoons.

No, she was nothing at all like her mother. She didn't believe in boys who came from *elsewhere*. She simply refused.

2

*In which Ophelia, while refusing to save
the world, does something very brave indeed*

———◆———

Miss Kaminski was tall and elegant in a crisp white pant-suit. She stood in the doorway to the sword workroom and smiled a dazzling smile. Mr. Whittard, looking up from his station, magnifying glass and lamp in his white-gloved hands, turned red at the sight of her.

"I have been thinking," said Miss Kaminski. "Perhaps Miss Alice and Miss Cordelia would like a special tour of the museum."

"Ophelia," whispered Ophelia.

Miss Kaminski looked at Ophelia as though she had heard something but was not sure what it might be. She looked at her as though she were looking at something small and insignificant. Ophelia saw her gaze at Alice, who was sitting in the corner of the room, in an old throne, twirling her long blond hair and looking very bored.

"Miss Alice looks like a girl who would be interested in jewels," said Miss Kaminski.

Alice, reclining on frayed cushions, looked very uninterested. She held up a section of her hair and examined its end, and stared straight through Miss Kaminski as though she weren't there at all.

"Wigs, shoes, dresses?" said Miss Kaminski. "Dolls, music boxes, mirrors? Mazes, the customs of love, Oriental textiles, white horses with wings made of marble, lipsticks, the history of dance, violins, piccolos?"

Alice continued staring at a point past Miss Kaminski's head. She was being quite rude.

"The dresses," continued Miss Kaminski, "are some of the most beautiful and most expensive ever made in the world. I would love for you to see these things, Alice."

"I guess," said Alice at last.

"And Miss Cordelia," said Miss Kaminski.

"Ophelia."

"I think you look like a girl who would like very much to see . . ."

"Dinosaurs," said Ophelia.

Miss Kaminski led them through the galleries, and in and out of the silver staff-only elevators. She looked back at them from time to time, smiled, beckoned them on. Ophelia did not like her, although she couldn't say why. If she was to think about it, logically, Miss Kaminski looked like a model in a magazine and she smelt very nice. Both of these things should have made her agreeable. Yet every time Ophelia was near her, she felt worried. She was worried in a nameless, shapeless, strange way, which, however hard she tried, she couldn't put her finger on. Walking behind Miss Kaminski,

Ophelia had to pull on her braids again to make herself feel better.

Miss Kaminski took them first to the *Gallery of Time*, and the crowd parted in two waves before her. The Wintertide Clock was as tall as the ceiling and its face as white as snow. Its hands were silver and dangerously sharp. It ticked so loudly that Ophelia could feel its mechanics inside her and through the soles of her feet.

Around the perimeter of the clock face, there were smaller clock faces, and when Ophelia peered closer, she saw that within these smaller clocks, there were even tinier timepieces.

"The Wintertide Clock is the most important piece in the museum and one of the most important clocks in the world," Miss Kaminski said, and although she spoke only to Alice, the crowd grew hushed. "It has over seven hundred moving wheels and cogs, and keeps time to the movement of the stars and the moon."

Miss Kaminski pointed to the many clock faces with one elegant sweep of her arm.

"Standing here, I can tell the time anywhere in the world. In Sofia or Saharanpur. In Mobile, Mito, and Mogadishu."

She spoke to the crowd now as well.

"But why does this remarkable clock chime only once every three hundred years? No one can remember now, but we know from records that the day is fast approaching. What song will its bells play us when it chimes? People, soon the world will understand its great mysteries.

"On Christmas Eve, *Battle: The Greatest Exhibition of Swords in the History of the World* will begin and will coincide with the opening of the Wintertide Clock's chime doors. We shall hear those chimes and understand this clock's true purpose."

Alice sighed and turned up the volume in her earphones.

Beneath the silver chime doors, Ophelia saw the little window that the boy had mentioned. It contained a very ornate number 3. She thought of the boy locked away in the loneliest part of the museum. She shook her head. Oh, how that boy, locked behind that door, made her feel unsettled. She felt her stomach twist itself in knots. He shouldn't have been there, and he shouldn't have spoken to her, and he shouldn't have asked her to save the world.

All this talk of wizards. If wizards were real, how could they take his name, however much it was attached to his soul, and hold it in their hands, as heavy as a stone? She tried to imagine explaining that at the Children's Science Society.

But if she retrieved the key for him, then she could at least say she had helped. She could probably find his name too. He probably hadn't even tried to think about it—really think, sit down with a freshly sharpened pencil and go through the alphabet, which would be the methodical, scientific thing to do. That was what you had to do in those sort of situations.

If she could let him out and help him find his name, then at least he might be able to get home. Once they had his name, first name and surname, then they could go through the phone book. There was bound to be one somewhere.

Adam, Ophelia thought, just to get started while they walked along. Alphonse, Abelard, Abernathy, Aaron, Abdul.

Abraham, Adolf, Adrian, Albert, Alexander. She needed a piece of paper. She could sit down with him. They'd cross off the names that meant nothing to him and circle the ones that felt familiar. Surely it wouldn't be so hard to find the right one.

Miss Kaminski led them through many galleries. She showed them an urn made out of beetle shells.

Axel, Ophelia thought, feeling positive. Addison, Ainsley, and Aristotle.

Miss Kaminski then led them through a room filled with carnival masks and another filled with crowns.

Ajay, Alan, Alastair, thought Ophelia, still upbeat.

Miss Kaminski showed them both the great staircase and the lesser staircases and the golden arcade, where the ceiling was studded with precious stones.

Andrew, Ambrose, Archie. A little less happy.

She had put her hand in her pocket to retrieve her puffer, and when she did, the little hole ripped into an even bigger hole. She caught her puffer just as it was about to fall through. She placed it in the left-hand pocket and knew she would never be able to use the right-hand pocket again. It made her feel very despondent to be a one-pocketed girl.

Aladdin, Albie, Alex, Alf . . . actually quite downcast.

All the way through the teaspoon gallery . . . downright glum.

Suddenly Miss Kaminski stopped. To her horror Ophelia saw they were standing on the sea monster mosaic. Ophelia retrieved her inhaler and puffed. Miss Kaminski cocked her head just a little, as though she were listening for something.

"I've always felt this is one of the least interesting sections of the museum," she said, before continuing on.

In the dinosaur hall, the huge ceiling arched overhead. It was all wrought iron and skylights covered in snow. The place danced with shadows and was alive with echoes. The walls turned even the smallest of whispers into shouts. It was a cold, murky place. The guard woke in the corner on her chair and began to knit furiously.

"There are hours of amusement here," said Miss Kaminski, standing in the gloom beneath the giant skeleton of a *Brachiosaurus*. Her sentence was repeated by the walls several times. "There are the dinosaurs, of course, and in these cabinets, some of the most remarkable fossils in the world. I will show Alice some wonderful dresses, and we shall return for you in one hour."

"Thank you," said Ophelia.

And the walls said, *Thank you, thank you, thank you.*

"Do not go anywhere else," said Miss Kaminski.

"I won't," promised Ophelia.

I won't, I won't, I won't.

Miss Kaminski patted her on the head. She meant it kindly, but Ophelia noticed the distaste in the museum curator's eyes, as though she were patting a small toad.

Ophelia waited until they had gone. The guard lowered the knitting to her lap and went back to sleep. There was one other person in the hall. An old man. He stood for so long, bent over a small pile of bones in a glass box, that Ophelia thought perhaps he had come yesterday and frozen solid there.

She quivered with the cold. The shadows of birds moved above the snow-covered skylights.

The old man finally creaked upright, looked at her sternly, and left through the darkened door.

Ophelia walked around the *Brachiosaurus* and *Tyrannosaurus rex*. *Triceratops* was starting to crumble, and some bones lay scattered on the floor beneath it. No one had bothered to pick them up. Barry, she tried. Bartholemew, Baxter, Bert, Bob, but without much conviction. She peered into the gloomy, dark cases at the strange collections of bones. She walked round and round the great room. Past the guard, past the fossils, past the dinosaurs. Each time she went round the hall, she tried to ignore the small elevator the boy had mentioned standing in a darkened alcove humming quietly to itself. She walked round and round the room until her legs ached.

The elevator doors had a large cross painted upon them, which could only mean "Do not enter." Each step Ophelia took, the panic rose inside her.

You are too young to worry so, her mother said, suddenly inside her mind. It was exactly what her mother always said.

"That's all right for you to say," replied Ophelia silently and quite angrily. "You haven't got a boy that needs to be rescued."

More than anything, she felt annoyed at the boy for appearing behind that door and knowing her name and asking for her help.

"I'm not brave enough," Ophelia said aloud, and the walls whispered, whispered, whispered. The guard did not wake up. Ophelia Jane Worthington-Whittard looked at the guard sleeping and looked at the dinosaurs and walked very quietly up to the elevator.

She pressed the large round silver button, and the doors slid open.

She stepped inside. It was deathly still. The lightbulb flickered.

She pressed the button engraved with the number 7.

The elevator opened onto the seventh floor, into a huge room that was empty and cold. There were no statues or artwork, just the white marble floor weaved with silver. The windows, covered in delicate, spidery patterns of ice, looked out over the city square and the giant sparkling Christmas tree.

There was not a sound in that room. The silence buzzed in her ears. Her boots made a terrible clatter on the floor and her breath plumed in front of her. She trembled with fear.

On either side of the immense, empty room there was a doorway that led onto a corridor. She walked as quickly as she could across the expanse of empty marble floor to the left-hand corridor. She pulled her blue velvet coat collar up and put her hands in her pockets. Her teeth chattered.

On either side of the left-hand corridor there were rooms. Each room had a number above it in silver. She touched the handles lightly. The doors were locked.

The corridor had a very strange smell. It took her all the time to walk to room number 716 to remember what it was. It was exactly the smell of Mr. Fleming's pigeon coop at 7 Bedford Gardens. Mr. Fleming lived right beside the

Whittard-Worthingtons in Kensington, London, and Ophelia could speak to him over the back fence if she stood on a garden chair. He bred and raced Danzig highflyers and blue dragoons, and he was very kind to Ophelia, sometimes opening the little gate between their gardens so she could look at the newly hatched chicks.

Yes, it was just the same here, a dank, moldy, feathery type of smell. There must be pigeons living in the ceiling, Ophelia thought, and then shivered. Her chin went numb with the cold. Her ears ached.

The corridor turned just after room number 721. She was surprised to see that at the end of the passage, not very far away, there was a small white cupboard against a blank white wall.

She felt very pleased. The whole exercise had been easier than she expected. The little white cupboard had only one little white drawer. She opened it very quietly and saw one small golden key. Everything was exactly as the boy had said it would be.

She took the key and put it in her blue velvet coat pocket. Her favorite right-hand coat pocket. She smiled to herself. She smiled to herself because the day had turned out to be very interesting and she had turned out to be really quite brave. The key fell through her right-hand pocket hole and clattered onto the floor.

There was silence at first, then a rustling, sighing, swishing, hushing sound.

The rustling, sighing, swishing, hushing sound was small

to start off, but then it grew louder. It grew so loud that it was the only sound that Ophelia could hear.

The sound came from behind the doors.

Then another noise. A noise more terrible than the first. The sound of something very sharp on the marble floor.

A *click, clack.*

A *scritch, scratch.*

The sound of talons.

The distinct sound of claws.

Ophelia scooped up the key and began to run. She ran and did not look back. She turned the corner and sped toward the elevator, waiting with its open mouth. Each room she passed, the sound grew louder. The click, clack, rustle, sigh, scratch, and now the rattling of the doorknobs. Something was trying to escape. She slipped on the marble floor in the large open room, skidded on her denim bottom into the elevator, scrambled onto her knees, slammed the number 3 with her fist, and fell backward as the door closed.

3

*In which Miss Kaminski returns for Ophelia
and looks at her suspiciously*

———◆———

O phelia could not breathe. She couldn't breathe when she
stepped out of the elevator. She couldn't breathe when she
stood pretending to carefully study *Triceratops*. She couldn't
breathe when Alice and Miss Kaminski returned for her.

She took a squirt on her puffer.

Then another.

"Are you okay?" said Alice.

"Yes," squeaked Ophelia.

"You're as cold as ice," said Alice, touching her sister's cheek.

She wrapped her scarf around Ophelia's neck. It reminded
Ophelia of the old Alice. The Alice before their mother was
ill. The Alice who took the stairs three at a time and sang
into her hairbrush and laughed loudly on the phone to her
friends. The Alice who held Ophelia's hand and lent her hair-
clips and offered kind and well-meant, if not utterly useless,
fashion advice.

Ophelia could feel the key heavy in her left pocket, where she had carefully stowed it. She was sure Miss Kaminski must be aware of it. Surely there was a light shining from her pocket announcing to the world that she, Ophelia, was a thief.

Miss Kaminski looked at her rather suspiciously. She bent down and touched Ophelia's cheeks with her very cold hands, which only made her feel more freezing.

"Look," said Alice, and she turned her head to show an antique lace flower clip in her long blond hair. "Miss Kaminski said I could borrow it from the collection."

Alice had put away her headphones. Her cheeks were flushed. She pointed to a little pink diamond brooch on her coat lapel and held out a turquoise ring on her finger.

Miss Kaminski smiled. The museum curator knelt down in front of Ophelia. "And did you enjoy the dinosaurs, Miss Amelia?" she asked.

"Oh yes," Ophelia squeaked again, too scared to correct Miss Kaminski. "I did very much."

Miss Kaminski deposited the sisters in the sword workroom and did not stay long. She said she was continuing preparations for the greatest and most remarkable sword of all to be unlocked from its city vault in two days' time to take its place of pride in the exhibition.

"Mr. Whittard, when you see this sword, your heart will stop," Miss Kaminski said.

Ophelia watched her father try to speak in the presence of the beautiful museum curator. He nodded, fumbled with his glasses, then managed to knock over a cup filled with pens. Alice sighed loudly. As soon as Miss Kaminski was gone, Ophelia jumped up.

"I have to go somewhere," she said.

"Aren't we going skating?" shouted Alice.

"I won't be too long," said Ophelia, already halfway up the stairs.

She ran through the galleries until she found the narrow corridor that led to the room filled with teaspoons. Her feet led her then. Through the telephones, the mirrors, the elephants, the wolves. She slipped through the crowd ogling the Wintertide Clock in the *Gallery of Time*. She raced down the hallway filled with gloomy paintings of girls.

She stopped there because she was out of breath.

And because she thought it must be sad to be a painting of a girl that no one ever stopped to look at.

She walked slowly down the corridor, gazing at each girl or almost every girl—there were so many of them, and they all looked very similar. They were all very pretty, and they all looked very disappointed. She saw that at the bottom of each gold frame there was a name.

Tess Janson, Katie Patin, Matilda Cole, Johanna Payne, Judith Pickford, Millie Mayfield, Carys Sprock, Sally Temple-Watts, Paulette Claude, Kyra Marinova, and Amy Cruit. She stopped reading after that because she'd got her breath back.

"Goodbye, Amy Cruit," said Ophelia. "Can't stay. Got to rush."

* * *

"Breathe," said the boy through the keyhole.

Ophelia knelt with her hands on her knees.

"There are things up there on the seventh floor," she said finally.

"Of course there are things up there," the boy replied.

"But what sort of things are they?" said Ophelia angrily.

"They're the misery birds," he said. "They are a type of bird and a type of monster. You're very brave."

"You should have told me they were up there."

"I did tell you they were up there. You didn't believe me."

Ophelia shivered. She was just beginning to thaw. She rubbed her hands together, cupped them over her mouth, and breathed into them. She looked through the keyhole.

"I'm not meant to have bad frights," she said. "It's my asthma."

"Did you get the key?" asked the boy.

"Yes," she said, and slipped it from her pocket. She went to place it in the lock hidden in the door of the turquoise sea.

"No," said the boy. "It doesn't open that."

"Pardon?" Now Ophelia felt really cross.

"This key opens a small box on the sixth floor. I haven't seen it, so I cannot say at all what it looks like, but I know it's there."

"How do you know?" asked Ophelia. The mention of a floor so close to the seventh made her queasy. Suppose those miserable birds woke up again? What must they look like if just the sound of them had made her hair stand on end?

"Mr. Pushkinova has told me some. He is the keeper of

the Queen's keys, and while he has guarded this cell for many years, he has always been very kind to me. Also there is Mrs. V., who does the cleaning and sometimes brings me breakfast and supper. She never says much, but when she does, it is very useful. She has been coming for seventy years, almost as long as Mr. Pushkinova. And before Mrs. V., there were others. I have gathered the information over many years. You must go to the sixth floor and find the box and open it with this key. There will be another key inside."

"Seventy years? But you don't look any older than me," said Ophelia.

"I am much older," said the boy. "I began my journey three hundred and three years ago. It is only as a result of a blessing bestowed on me by a great magical owl that I shot through the heart with my arrow that I appear this way."

"Now you're really being silly."

But she looked through the keyhole at his clothes. She had to admit they were very old-fashioned-looking. His coat was embroidered with gold birds with emerald eyes. It must have once been a splendid thing. Now it was unraveling at the sleeves.

"The things I could tell you," he said quietly.

He was looking away, she could see, looking intently at his hands, perhaps to hide his disappointment. It made her feel terrible, such talk: wizards and magical owls and arrows through the heart. But he looked so sad and lonely.

Ophelia Jane Worthington-Whittard crossed her arms. "Tell me, then," she said.

And so the boy began.

* * *

I ran the way the wizards had always shown me. Well, I mean, they always showed me the way by walking—they don't run, as such; their bones are too rickety. They always took me out through the south gate and then through the fields and into the forest. They said if I followed the compass south, I would pass through the belly of the mountain and then across the sea. I would go through the meridian, the point of no return. They never told me how I was expected to cross the sea, even when I asked. When I got to the other side, I would find a just and noble king.

So that was the way I went, out through the south gate and through the fields, which were covered in frost. There were people everywhere that morning, people with their whole lives tied up and teetering on top of wagons, heading out of the kingdom to escape the Snow Queen's invasion. And everywhere there were boys and men rushing this way and that with their horses and their newly forged swords. But that is another story.

I didn't want anyone to see me that morning. I didn't want them to shout, "Ay, there's the boy chosen by the wizards, running in the wrong direction, away from the Snow Queen. How will that help us, boy?" I slipped into the rows of frosted corn as quickly as I could and then soon into the forest.

The quiver, even though it only held one arrow, hurt my back. And the sword! It was so heavy. It banged against my thigh and made it ache. And I stepped in a puddle and my shoes got wet, and I knew right away they'd dry and give me blisters.

I ran the way the wizards and I had walked in the forest together. Keeping close to the stream and then crossing it where the great oaks stood. Running and running until I touched the first of the Herald Trees.

Why are you looking at me like that, Ophelia? Surely they are in your scientific books? Herald Trees are the messenger trees, terribly magical. Wizards talk for miles through them.

I stopped at the Herald Tree, trying to catch my breath, and when I stopped, all I could hear was my breathing. The whole forest was still, still, still.

And I put my hand to the tree's trunk as I'd been taught, and separated out all the parts of the day, the quiet grass whispering and the stream chattering, until I came upon the sound of emptiness. And in that space all I heard, suddenly, was the Great Wizard's voice, shouting, "Run—you must run, boy!" And then the grating, scraping sound of a sleigh and the clamor of swords.

So I began to run again.

The Snow Queen's army had arrived in the town. I knew it then, from the little I had heard. They would be meeting the first line of defense in the fields: the plodding brown farm horses; the young boys, their faces turned white with fear. In the legends the winter soldiers had pale blue eyes and skin like marble and hair the color of dead marsh reed. And now I imagined they would be drawing their swords and ending everyone they met, no matter how much they cowered and begged in the streets. Then they would begin to look for me.

They would stand in darkened houses and sniff the air; they would pick apart locks with their fingernails.

I could not know it then, but that very moment, they were releasing three great magical owls from their chains. Ibrom was among them. He was the owl that would take my finger and put the charm on me. I could not know it, for I was in the forest running. I was running, and my back was aching, and my thigh was aching from where the sword hit me every step. There were blisters forming on my feet. I ran and ran and ran.

It isn't fair was what I thought. I hadn't even eaten breakfast. I hadn't said goodbye to my mother, not properly. Why hadn't I said, *I love you?* I thought of the biscuits Petal had packed me and then of the food my mother had placed in the satchel. The bread and cheese. That's such a simple thought, isn't it? In a world about to be torn apart by the Snow Queen. But it made me stop. That thought stopped me in my tracks. I stopped running; I sat down on the ground. I began to cry. I cried for the wizards who had chosen the wrong person, and I cried for the town folk, who would surely be meeting their end, and I cried for my mother. How I cried for her. The tears fell down my cheeks and onto my hands. I wiped my nose on my sleeve. The spell that coated me began to wash away. And high above the forest, the great magical owl, Ibrom, caught my scent.

Ophelia looked through the keyhole at the boy then. She bit her bottom lip. It was terrible to imagine him all alone in the forest, crying, the spell dripping from him with his tears. But even worse to imagine something hunting him.

"How did the Snow Queen's soldiers know about you?" she asked, to change the subject. "I mean, how did they know to look for you in particular?"

She liked her stories to be factual and very organized.

But he didn't answer. "It's getting late. See, the sun is starting to set," he said. "If you're to find the second key, you must go soon or it will be too dark in the forest."

"Forest?" said Ophelia, and when the boy didn't answer again, she added, "It wasn't right of them anyway. To send you off like that. And to take your name. Everyone needs a name."

"I got used to it after a while."

"Have you tried going through the alphabet?"

"Yes."

"I tried it earlier," said Ophelia. "I only did *A* and *B*. I'm sure we could find your name if we did that. I'll bring some paper and pencil next time."

"So, the second key," said the boy.

Ophelia looked at the mural of the boy. He was holding his raised sword out in front of him. It was a large sword with a wooden hilt, and it was otherwise plain, except for a little carving of a closed eye. It didn't look very magical.

What will you do? She heard her mother's voice clear in her ear.

"The problem is I've already stolen once today," said Ophelia, who had never stolen before. The first key burnt in her left-hand pocket.

She saw the boy smile through the keyhole, and she noticed the dimple again. When he moved a little, she caught a glimpse of the dim room. A small bed. A plain table with a bowl and pitcher. A small, high window with a thin slant of late-afternoon light and snow.

"Did you look at the Wintertide Clock?" the boy asked.

"There was a number three," said Ophelia.

"Three days!" said the boy. "That soon? We don't have much time."

Ophelia took off her smudgy glasses and began to clean them on her coat hem. "What happens in three days?" she asked tentatively, although she would rather not have asked at all.

"Unless we find the sword and the One Other," said the boy, "in three days' time, I will die and the Snow Queen will be victorious. I am a boy chosen by a protectorate of wizards from east, west, and the middle to deliver this sword so that the Snow Queen may be defeated."

Ophelia looked at the floor. She looked at the snow falling outside the window. She felt embarrassed. Apart from his golden coat, he really looked like only a scruffy boy.

"Well, I've probably been gone a long time," she said. "My father will be looking for me."

"Ophelia," said the boy. He said it very quietly. She didn't like the way he said that at all. He sounded sad and as though he expected more from her.

"And how do you know my name anyway?" she said. "I never told you it, not once."

"I heard it once, a long time ago."

He was full of mysterious sentences like that. She pulled down on her braids.

"I really should be going. Alice gets so cross nowadays," she said.

"Will you come back?"

"I'll try."

"One thing," said the boy as she started to turn. "If you go to the sixth floor, be careful. There are ghosts there, dangerous ghosts."

Ophelia rolled her eyes. She didn't turn back.

"Be careful not to tell them too much about yourself!" he shouted as she left the room.

Which, as far as she was concerned, didn't make any sense at all.

4

*In which Ophelia decides she does not believe
in ghosts and visits the sixth floor*

———◆———

Ghosts, thought Ophelia. She went out through the stone angels and across the sea monster mosaic. She walked down the long gallery of the gloomy paintings of girls, past Amy Cruit and Millie Mayfield and Paulette Claude. She stopped reading their names after that.

Ghosts, she thought again. Where was the evidence for ghosts?

After her mother died, Ophelia had crept into her study each morning and sat in her mother's writing chair. She'd touched her desk, her pen, the vampire teeth. She'd taken the *Encyclopaedia of Ghosts and Spirits* from her mother's bookcase. Each morning she opened it to a different page. There were fetches and bhoots and doppelgängers. Spooks and wraiths and gjengangers. Intelligent hauntings, shadow ghosts, funnel ghosts, poltergeists. Wouldn't her mother try to contact her, if it was all true? Wouldn't she come and sit on the end of her bed or lift a curtain or hide her toothbrush?

Her mother did none of these things. When Ophelia sat in her mother's chair, there was just a light-filled emptiness. A nothingness. A silence that made her so sad that she couldn't even cry. A sadness that sat on her chest and crushed the air out of her with its weight.

Ghosts, Ophelia thought again, in the pavilion of wolves. She looked at the poor things, with their mangy, moth-eaten coats and their dull glass eyes. An ancient guard watched her without any interest and went back to eating a very old apple.

Ophelia looked at the silver elevator in the corner of the room. She chewed on a fingernail for a while before taking a puff on her inhaler. She pressed the UP button then and tried to ignore the sinking feeling in her stomach.

The first thing Ophelia noticed about floor six was a giant polar bear standing on its hind legs, its mouth open in a silent roar. Her heart stopped momentarily and then started beating again. The second thing she noticed was that the sixth floor was not really part of the museum at all but a place where everything that didn't have a home was kept.

She squeezed herself past the polar bear, picked her way past a tower of sewing machines, several large printing presses, a locomotive, two huge jars filled with buttons, a pile of suit-cases, fountains of gowns draped over antique chairs, mounds of handbags, and several merry-go-round horses staring at her with their melancholy eyes.

"Ghosts," she said aloud with disdain.

It wasn't a frightening place at all. It was just a forgotten place. A little like a box of old toys pushed under a bed, only on a grander scale. These strange, mismatched collections stretched as far as she could see. There were flags of the world, snow shakers, artwork stacked in teetering heaps, newspapers, books, and three grand pianos. There were grandfather clocks, a Morse code machine, a ship's huge anchor, a century of golfing attire, several stuffed parrots. There were display cabinets without displays, displays without display cabinets.

Ophelia found a bridal veil and placed it on her head.

She pressed the letter *O* three times on an ancient typewriter.

She took the veil off. She retrieved the key from her pocket.

"Okay, a box, a box that this key opens," she said into the gloom. Her shoulders slumped.

She worked her way back to the polar bear and started again. She looked for locks of any sort. She tried the key inside an antique sewing box, a toolbox on the floor of the locomotive; she tried several stout writing desks. She was briefly excited when she came upon a small pile of lacquered jewelry boxes, but the key opened none of them. It was too big, by far.

She started again. It was a room full of objects, but almost none of them were locked. Almost none of them were boxes. It was very, very frustrating.

Slow down, she heard her mother say, quite close to her ear. *Slow down and really look.*

Ophelia waved her hand as if at a worrisome fly. She could sense the sun was setting now. The light had changed behind the grimy windows. Her stomach grumbled. Alice would be quite mad. She'd be waiting on the throne with their ice skates and a frown on her face. Ophelia longed for her old sister, the old Alice, who was carefree and funny and who never frowned.

Ophelia stopped and looked exceedingly slowly. Immediately she noticed the door near a silver carriage strung with spiderwebs. It was at the very back of the huge room. Of course, she thought, there wouldn't be only one room on the sixth floor. There would be several rooms. Behind this door there were probably many boxes. There would be boxes in piles, heaps, mountains, oodles of boxes stacked up in pyramids. She reached out for the doorknob and opened the door.

Behind the door there were no oodles of boxes. There were no boxes at all. Ophelia stepped into a room that was vast and almost in darkness. There was nothing in this room but huge pillars, evenly spaced, disappearing into the dark above her.

It *was* like a forest, that room, but it didn't sing and rustle like an ordinary forest. It was quiet and the only noise was the slight creaking of the floor beneath her feet. It was much colder in that room than in the first. She pulled her coat collar up as she began to walk and wished she had a flashlight. There was something falling from the heights above her. Dust, she thought at first, white dust, and she put her hand out to catch some. The stuff was wet on her palm, which was confusing, and if she'd been outside, she would have said straightaway that it was snow.

Ophelia Jane Worthington-Whittard did not consider herself brave, but she had always been very hopeful. "Anything is possible if you have a plan" was her motto. "Anything is possible if you think scientifically." It made her smile now, in the darkened room.

Of course, behind this room, there would be another room filled with boxes. She would search it in a grid pattern, which was exactly how archaeologists and police officers found things. She would search it slowly and methodically. She might even find the old sword while she was there. And the One Other, whoever that was, if it was even someone at all. Some more of the wet white stuff fell from the ceiling, but it didn't dampen her enthusiasm. There was a strange smell tickling her nose, a singed kind of smell, a little like burnt popcorn.

She walked through the forest of pillars. She walked and walked, and there did not seem to be an end to that room. She thought of the boy's name to pass the time. Colin, she thought. No, not Colin, that was silly. Christopher. Crawford. Conan. Clyde, Clive, Cameron, Carl, Cassidy. Surely one of the names would jump out at her, and she would know. There was a noise. A whispering, rustling type of sound and it seemed to come from beneath her feet. She bent down and felt with her hands in the dim and picked up a pile of dark leaves.

"That's very strange," said Ophelia.

And at exactly the same time, she heard another sound. It might have been the wind or the sighing of snow through the leaves, only it was very close to her ear. And the sound that might have been the wind or the sighing of snow through the leaves suddenly became a multitude of girls' voices, whispering very close to her.

You are safe here, they said. *The wolves do not like us, the owls do not like us. The white horses will not come here, nor the white lions. They will never, ever, ever, ever enter here. They are afraid of us. Are you here for the box with the second key?*

It was the soft, rushing, sighing, singing, whispering of voices.

"Who are you?" shouted Ophelia, spinning around, the leaves falling through her fingers.

No answer. In the silence she heard someone giggle.

What is your name? the voices asked, a blustery, blowing circle of voices. *What is your name? No one has tried for so long. We have been waiting and waiting and waiting and waiting.*

"Who are you?" shouted Ophelia again.

We are many, said the voices. *We are the children. We belong to the Queen.*

"Can one of you speak alone?" demanded Ophelia. "You're hurting my ears."

The voices sped away then. She felt the breath of their departure. She didn't know that those ghosts couldn't bear to be apart. That all night they lay in tangles, waiting, combing each other's hair with their fingers, touching each other's words and stories, going over and over them, whispering into each other's ears.

She felt them move away from her, pacing, then running, barreling at breakneck speed, and then they were turning, rushing back toward her.

We are Millie, who liked to run; we could run like the wind, said the voices. *We are Katie, who liked to climb in the apple tree. We are Paulette, and our mother had hands that were pink and soft. They sat in her lap, just like this. We are so lonely.* They wept suddenly.

"What are you doing here?" whispered Ophelia.

We've already told you, said the voices. *You are safe with us. Please tell us your story.*

But Ophelia didn't feel safe with them. Not really. She remembered now what the boy had told her. *Be careful not to tell them too much about yourself.* She felt tiny things touching her. It was as if she were walking through a spiderweb. She wiped at her face and put her hands out before her. The ghost girls whispered and whispered and whispered.

"It's very rude to whisper so," said Ophelia, shivering in the cold, dim air. The white stuff was falling solidly now, exactly like snow.

The voices grew clearer and closer again.

We think you should stay here with us, they said quite loudly. *Here is safe. Here is good. Nothing can harm you. There is no harm here. Would you like to play with us? We have much to tell you. Can't you stay awhile? We can make you warm. We can make you happy. Are you listening?*

"Thank you," said Ophelia. "But I'm very busy. I have to get back as soon as possible. I have to go ice-skating."

I have to go ice-skating. They mimicked her voice.

A thunderclap of laughter.

The ghost girls stopped being so polite. They touched

her with their invisible hands, little fluttering touches. One brushed her face. One kissed her cheek. She felt an icy breath there. Something touched her back. Someone pulled her braid.

We think you are wrong, they said. *Wrong, wrong, wrong. We think you should stay and play games. That boy can never be rescued. His charm will be broken, and he will be gone, and he will be dead and buried. The Queen will rule the world.*

The voices circled her now. Someone very rough pushed her to the ground on her knees. Her glasses fell off—she felt for them in the dark in the leaves.

Leave her alone, came one voice from the invisible crowd. *We shouldn't have done that.*

Ophelia pulled herself up, her glasses in her hand. She checked to see that she still had the key.

"Who are you?" she asked, but there was no reply.

"The one who said, 'Leave her alone'?" she asked again.

Nothing.

A low whispering.

Careful, Kyra, said the voices.

We are Kyra, said the voice of Kyra, very softly.

Careful, whispered the voices together again.

She cannot harm us, said Kyra.

We are all for one and one for all, said the ghost girls.

Kyra did not move closer.

"Kyra?" said Ophelia. "How did you come here?"

We were a girl just like you, said Kyra. *Then we were stolen and put in the Queen's machine so she could be full of strength and live forever. All that was left of us was given to this dark place.*

The agony, moaned the children together.

"The machine?" said Ophelia.

Oh, the agony, moaned the children even louder.

She took so much of us that we must always stay together or we fade, said Kyra. *And we have to remind each other who we are or we fade, and we cannot go near the light or we fade. Our stories make us strong.*

Our stories make us strong, recited the voices. *Tell us your story.*

And we cannot look at the light, said Kyra, *or it will tear us apart.*

There is no light, thought Ophelia, and she fancied turning back because she suddenly felt so cold and hungry and alone, even though she was surrounded by the voices. But the thought of walking back the way she had come, with these ghostly companions, was unbearable, and surely she was closer now to the end of the room than the beginning. She felt Kyra then, close beside her, breathing right into her ear, and the singed popcorny smell of her tickled her nose.

Tell us a little, said Kyra, but then she whispered, *but not too much or we'll gobble you up, and it will not be our fault.*

Where is Kyra? asked the chorus of voices. *Stand with us, sister.*

And Kyra disappeared from Ophelia's side again.

Tell us your story, demanded the ghost girls.

"Well, my name is Ophelia," she said. "Ophelia Jane Worthington-Whittard and I was born in Wandsworth, but later we moved to Kensington. I have a sister called Alice.

She's very pretty. And a father; his name is Malcolm. And a mother, or I had a mother, but she died. Her name was Susan. But anyway, my father came here to put together an exhibition. It's called *Battle: The Greatest Exhibition of Swords in the History of the World.* I don't know if you've heard of it. And he has to get it ready in only three days because something happened to the last sword expert—I'm not sure what. He had to leave or something. My father knows everything about swords. Absolutely everything."

These are not the stories we wish to hear, whispered the voices, very close. *Who was your mother?* they asked in unison, stroking her hair. *Tell us your story,* they said, fiddling with her buttons. *What did she sing to you at night? What did she say to you in the morning? Did she ever dance you on the top of her shoes?*

Careful, whispered Kyra in her ear.

Stand with us, sister! shouted the voices, and Kyra was gone again.

"Why don't you tell me *your* stories?" said Ophelia, heeding Kyra's warning.

There was a brief silence before a cacophony of whispers.

Who are we, who are we, who are we? whispered the voices. *We are Matilda. Our father was big as a mountain. We are Tess. We were apprenticed to the illuminator. We are Greer. Our mother had golden hair.* All around her, Ophelia heard the memories recited. *We loved to dance. We loved to sing. We loved to walk on the dew. We loved to leave our footprints in the snow. We are Kara. We are Sally. We are Mira. We had green eyes. Our father could hold us in the palm of his hand, so small were we. We could hold our breath underwater to the count of ten. We are Judith. We are Johanna. We are Carys.*

Finally, close, *We are Kyra. We lived in an apartment quite close to here. On the snowy streets, in the snowy city. Oh, but we had hair like fire.*

Ophelia felt an arm loop inside of hers. The tiniest breath of a voice.

I will help you, Kyra said. *There is not far to go now, but the way is treacherous.*

Ophelia became aware of a light, a distant glimmer. Its appearance seemed to distress the ghost girls. They moaned and cried.

Do not look forward, they said. *Look away, look away. The light will take you into the sky.*

But Kyra stayed close by her side.

"Are you looking at it?" whispered Ophelia.

Of course not, said Kyra.

But as she moved toward the light, Ophelia noticed that it was only the outline of a light shining from behind a door. "It's a door," she said. "Nothing else. It's just another room."

But how the ghost children lamented and cried.

Turn away, they cried. *Kyra, we must go. Turn back, turn back, do not look at the light.*

We are going to help her, said Kyra. Then, as though she had to think of the right word, *I am going to help her.*

Which caused great torment. A great moaning and crying and wailing.

On the other side of the light, there are the snow leopards, said Kyra into Ophelia's ear, *and they will tear you to shreds without me.*

"But what will happen to you?"

I am already dead, said Kyra.

They were close to the door now, and the ghost girls were shouting at the sheer calamity.

You will not leave us, they said. *No one leaves us. We will miss you too much. You must remain. Kyra, we are all for one and one for all.*

But Ophelia felt Kyra close by her side. She felt the other children, their running, their voices spinning in eddies. They weren't bad, Ophelia knew. Just very, very lonely.

Before the door, she asked, "Why?"

I would like to leave the forest, said Kyra, *just for a minute and run in the light without fear.*

And all around her the ghosts recited their stories loudly to blot out her heresy. *We are Joan. We are the youngest of twelve. We are Beattie. We like to pretend we have wings. We are Nora. We lived in the little house beside the mill stream. We are Valda. Our mother made dresses for the Queen. Do not look at the light. Do not look at the light. Do not look at the light. Do not look at the light. Do not look at the light.*

But Ophelia took a deep breath, and she felt Kyra do the same beside her, and she very calmly opened the door, and they stepped into the light-filled room.

It was a museum room, which made Ophelia extremely glad. A typical museum room, with a vast tiled floor and a seat in the middle for sitting on and admiring the paintings on the walls. These paintings were very large and mostly of a woman in a variety of white gowns and a variety of sparkling crowns. The woman looked vaguely familiar to Ophelia, with her brilliant blond hair and the cool smile on her face. She must have been someone famous. At each corner of the room, there was a white marble pillar, and atop each marble pillar, there was a stone snow leopard.

Ophelia knew they were snow leopards. Max Lowenstein had done a talk on them at the Children's Science Society of Greater London one Tuesday night. He was only eleven but knew everything there was to know about cats. These cats were smaller than the other great cats. They had domed heads and smallish ears and long, thick tails.

"Kingdom Animalia, phylum Chordata, class Mammalia, order Carnivora, family Felidae, subfamily Pantherinae, genus *Uncia*," said Ophelia. "But just statues. They're only statues."

Careful, said Kyra. *All is not as it seems.*

Ophelia spotted a box with a large keyhole on a small wooden table near another set of silver elevators.

"Where have you gone, Kyra?" she asked.

I am right here beside you, said Kyra. Yet her voice had grown very faint, as though she were a long way off. *Look now, they're waking.*

One of the stone snow leopards stopped being stone. Ophelia watched it in horror. It rose on its large paws and arched its back languidly, as though it had all the time in the world.

It dropped to the floor from the pillar with a dull thud.

"Impossible," whispered Ophelia. "They're moving."

I am right beside you, Kyra whispered back. *Quickly, ask me who I am. They'll not come near us if I stay strong.*

"Who are you?" said Ophelia. "Tell me something. What do you remember?"

I remember where I lived, a small place with a little window that looked out at the palace, and each morning, the snow.

One by one the three remaining snow leopards dropped to the floor. They did not roar—they made a low hissing noise as they moved toward Ophelia. Their yellow eyes gleamed, but they crouched suddenly at the sound of Kyra's voice. Ophelia backed slowly toward the table and the box.

"Tell me who you lived with."

I remember a man, a big, tall man with a large red beard.

One of the snow leopards took the lead. It stayed low to the ground, stalking, with its tail swishing behind. Ophelia knew it was waiting for the ghost girl to grow weak.

"Was the man your father?"

Yes, said the ghost girl.

"Tell me about him."

All four snow leopards crept forward, snarling. Ophelia could see their teeth, smell their breath. They hissed and chuffed and mewled. They sounded very hungry.

Don't look at them, said the ghost girl. *Only speak to me.*

"What did you like about him?"

I liked his hands. My two little hands could fit inside his, and sometimes he spun me around and around in the air.

"What else did you like about him?"

I liked his laugh. He had a laugh as big as he was, and when he laughed, it shook the room.

The leopards were so close that Ophelia could see herself reflected in their eyes. Still, they did not move forward while the ghost girl clung by her side.

We were poor. I didn't have fine clothes. Each morning I saw the Queen when she walked in her snow gardens, and each morning she looked up at me. She sent me a golden pear first, then a jewelry box, then she called for me.

Ophelia heard Kyra's voice strengthen beside her. Her voice was loud and close. The leopards stopped again, hunched, waiting to pounce.

I liked to write my name. I liked to write it again and again on the same piece of paper. I loved to run.

"And your hair was red?"

It was red as a flame. I had a scar on my cheek from when I fell from a chair and a burn on my hand from the frying pan.

Ophelia touched the table with her fingers. She reached behind her back for the box. The leopards let out a hiss and a wail. They bared their teeth.

"What happened when the Queen called you?"

She said, "I have seen you each day and been sorely amazed by your quaint prettiness. Look at your hair and your rosy cheeks, so full of life, exactly like a blossom. Do you remember these things?" Flowers, now, my father had told me of them.

I shivered in front of her in my little rag dress. She said, "I would like you to come with me. I have a special machine that will make you warm." And I followed her all the way up the steps, floors and floors and floors and floors, and all the courtiers and all the chambermaids came to watch her lead me.

Ophelia couldn't bear to hear the story, but she knew she

must listen or the leopards would have her. They scratched their claws along the marble floor and moved closer. Their tails lashed behind them.

They had smiles on their faces, you know, all those people. They knew exactly what would happen to me.

"What happened to you?"

The Queen put me in her machine. She said, "Kyra, there is nothing at all to fear." And that was the end of me.

Ophelia had the box in front of her now. It was a box painted with a winter scene. Her hands shook. She fumbled with the key—the lid opened on stiff hinges. Inside was a small copper key, very old, discolored green.

Quickly, you must go now, said Kyra, her voice suddenly weaker.

The lead snow leopard leapt toward Ophelia.

"Tell me what you loved!" Ophelia shouted just in time.

I loved to run. I could run forever, all the way through the streets until the fields began.

The leopard swerved, tumbled, crouched again on all fours.

"Come with me," Ophelia said, pressing the elevator button. She heard it rumbling away somewhere below.

But Kyra was fading.

"Tell me your name!" Ophelia shouted, stepping back into the elevator as the door opened.

My name was Kyra, Kyra said.

Ophelia saw her then, the outline of her. She saw her brilliant red hair. She burnt suddenly into existence in that museum gallery, the snow leopards poised behind her.

"Kyra!" she shouted as the elevator doors began to close.

You must go, Ophelia, Kyra said, her last words. She was unraveling. She burnt to life once more, and then there was nothing left of her.

The snow leopards leapt forward, the largest striking Ophelia across the sleeve as she fell backward. The snow leopard screeched as the doors shut on its powerful foreleg. It whined until it was free, and the doors closed completely. Ophelia scrambled into the far corner, pulled up her sleeve to see a thin line of blood. She put her head in her hands as the elevator began to descend.

5

*In which Miss Kaminski finds
Ophelia and is very cross*

———◆———

T he elevator opened onto the long, narrow gallery of
gloomy paintings of girls. It was very dark in that corridor; the sun must have set already, and all their quiet, lonely
faces were in shadow. Ophelia thought of the ghost girl, and it
made her so sad that she had to take her puffer from her pocket
and squirt.

She pulled up her sleeve again to look at her wound, which
was really only a scratch, but it made her feel terrible. What happened to scratches from magical snow leopards that changed
from stone to real living, breathing creatures in the blink of an
eye? Perhaps magical scratches were very bad. They might get
infected, and she might need to go to the hospital. How would
she explain it? No one at all would believe her.

And did she believe it herself?

Could statues really turn into real living, breathing snow
leopards? To prove they could, using the scientific method,

she would need to have a sample of snow leopard statues. She couldn't imagine explaining that one to the Children's Science Society of Greater London. Max Lowenstein would look at her as though she were from Mars. Maybe it was all a dream. Maybe she'd wake up soon. She pinched herself on her cheek to see.

Everything was too strange. It was giving her a terrible headache. She wished her mother were there. Her mother would know what to do. Her mother would say, "Now let's sit down and put our thinking caps on. Exactly what kind of monsters and mythical creatures are we dealing with?"

Ophelia knew she'd be in trouble. Her father would be angry because she'd been gone so long and Alice would have been waiting forever with their ice skates. She took another puff and tried to slow her breathing.

She read the names as she walked because it calmed her. There were Tess Janson and Katie Patin and Matilda Cole, and she peered at their faces in the dim light. Paulette Claude, Johanna Payne, Judith Pickford, Millie Mayfield, Harriet Springer, Carys Sprock, Kyra Marinova, Sally Temple-Watts, and Amy Cruit.

Kyra Marinova.

Ophelia walked backward, heart hammering. It just couldn't be.

Kyra Marinova.

She peered up at the face, the pale pretty face and the red ringlets and the quizzical expression. Two tears slid slowly down Ophelia's cheeks. She shivered and pulled her coat tighter. Felt the keys in her pocket. She didn't know what to believe anymore.

Ophelia ran then. She ran out of the gallery of painted girls, through the gilt rooms now filling up with night, along the great colonnade where the painted angels swam in the indigo gloom, past the paintings by the great masters, grown murky. All the guards had vacated their seats. They had packed up their knitting and zipped up their black handbags. The museum seemed completely empty.

But suddenly a whitish blur loomed out of the shadows.

"Miss Kaminski!" shouted Ophelia. "Oh, you gave me such a fright."

"Forgive me," said Miss Kaminski. The museum curator did not smile. "We have been looking everywhere for you. Your father has been very worried, and so have I."

"I got so lost," lied Ophelia. "I just . . ."

Miss Kaminski watched her face. She looked at where Ophelia was holding her arm.

"What has happened here?" asked the curator.

"I just . . ."

Miss Kaminski searched her eyes.

"What happened was . . . ," said Ophelia, hoping that Miss Kaminski wouldn't lift her sleeve and see the scratch.

Miss Kaminski took her by the elbow. Her fingernails were sharp, and even through the coat they pinched Ophelia. She felt suddenly very cold.

"Come," said Miss Kaminski. "I will take you to your father."

Down, down, down the damp, creaking stairs they went to

the sword workroom, where Alice was waiting with her skates in her hand. Ophelia's father was holding a medieval sword. Everywhere, men were lifting glass cases and carrying them out of the room under her father's direction.

"The wanderer has been found," said Miss Kaminski. She smiled now. She released her grip on Ophelia's elbow. A warm, sweet cloud of the curator's perfume washed over Ophelia.

"Ophelia!" said Mr. Whittard, embracing his daughter. "We were worried sick about you. I thought I told you to stay with Alice."

"Sorry," said Ophelia. "I just found so many interesting things, and then I got lost."

"She never does a thing I tell her," said Alice.

"Alice has been waiting all afternoon to take you ice-skating," said Mr. Whittard. "I'll have to stay here, I'm afraid. There is too much to be done. And apologize to Miss Kaminski, please. She hasn't got time to be running around the museum looking for you."

"I'm sorry, Miss Kaminski," said Ophelia.

Miss Kaminski smoothed Ophelia's hair across her brow. "All is forgiven," she said.

All the way through the museum, through the great foyer with its silvery wedding mosaic floor and its huge glittering chandeliers, Ophelia thought and thought and thought of the boy. I can unlock him from his room in the morning, she thought. Then I can help him find the sword. The magical snow leopard scratch ached on her arm. Ophelia and Alice walked through the giant revolving doors and out into the evening. I will help him to find the sword, and then that will be that. The rest he'll have to do by himself.

Outside, the cold stung their cheeks and their noses.

She thought of Kyra then, Kyra being led to the machine. That thought made her sadder than all the rest.

It made Ophelia cough, and Alice stopped and fixed her sister's scarf and beanie. The snow fell in dizzying flurries, and in the square, the Christmas tree—the largest Christmas tree Ophelia had ever seen—rustled and twinkled and tinkled with its thousands of silver bells and baubles.

Alice put on her skates and pushed off into the flow of skaters gliding around the rink, her long blond hair floating behind her. She had the antique lace rose in her hair and the brooch winking on her coat, and every now and again Ophelia saw her hold her hand up to look at the sparkling ring on her finger.

Alice came back to where Ophelia sat with her skates still in her hand.

"Why are you taking so long?" Alice asked.

"I'm just thinking," said Ophelia, looking across the square at the darkened museum. She lifted her hands up to her nose. She could still smell the leaves there, the damp, rotten leaves. She could still smell the girl, the girl who was a ghost. She touched her pocket with the two keys.

My little thinker, her mother whispered in her ear.

"You think too much," said Alice.

In the hotel room that night, Alice sat on the edge of Ophelia's bed. She removed Ophelia's glasses and put them on the nightstand. She kissed her on the cheek. She'd done that ever since their mother had died. But tonight her eyes were glassy.

"Your lips are like ice," said Ophelia.

Which made Alice laugh. Ophelia's sister looked out through the window beside them, where the snow fell and fell and fell and did not end. She smiled a strange faraway smile.

It was on the tip of Ophelia's tongue to ask her. Right there. Right then. To shout, "Alice, do you believe in magic?" But Ophelia didn't ask. She turned on her side instead, felt beneath the pillow for the keys, and then closed her eyes.

6

*In which Ophelia devises a plan and
is attacked by a Spanish conquistador*

———◆———

All night Ophelia slept with the two keys beneath her pillow. All night she tossed and turned, and her mother
spoke in her ear. *I like the story of the boy,* she said. *Imagine,
sent all that way to battle the Snow Queen. It's good and evil. You
know how I adore that sort of thing.* Ophelia covered her ears
with her hands. It was true; in all her mother's books, there
was someone good battling something very bad. And her bad
things were always very, very bad.

"Let me tell you a story," Ophelia's mother liked to say.
It was on the nights when Ophelia couldn't sleep, when her
asthma was bad and she had to be propped up on pillows.

"I'd rather you didn't."

"It isn't a terrifying one," her mother would say, slipping in
beside her.

But it would be.

"Can't you just tell me a simple fairy tale?" Ophelia
might plead.

"Oh, darling, fairy tales are for beginners," her mother would reply.

When she woke the next morning, Ophelia sat up and took the long gold key and the greenish plain key and held them in the palm of her hand. She looked out the window at the half-dark city, where the snow was falling.

What will you do? her mother asked her.

"Shoo," said Ophelia.

"Who are you talking to?" asked Alice, who was seated in front of the dressing table mirror, admiring her reflection.

"No one."

Alice placed a snow-white beret on her head and smiled at herself.

"Where did you get that hat from?" asked Ophelia.

"Miss Kaminski gave it to me."

"Why does Miss Kaminski keep giving you stuff?"

"Because she is very nice and very charming and absolutely fashionable."

Ophelia performed an exaggerated eye roll. *Very nice, very charming, absolutely fashionable,* she mimicked silently as she got dressed. She remembered how Miss Kaminski had pinched her through her coat last night. That wasn't very nice or very charming. Remembering, she looked at the wound on her arm, the long, thin scratch left behind by the snow leopard. She touched it gently with her fingertip. It ached and burned.

In the hotel suite lounge, Mr. Whittard was seated at the table with a pile of spreadsheets, his hair standing up on his head, his glasses perched on his forehead.

"Look at this," he said, pointing to a line of words when

75

Alice and Ophelia came out for breakfast. "I'm up to Teutonic long swords. I found one with a complete breastplate in a cardboard box. Can you believe that? Rare as hen's teeth."

Alice stared through him with her immaculately made-up eyes.

"I'm looking for a sword, actually," said Ophelia.

"Really, O," said Mr. Whittard. "What type of sword?"

"It's a very plain sword with a wooden hilt and a marking of a closed eye," said Ophelia. "And it's very magical."

"That's lovely, darling," said Mr. Whittard.

"It belonged to a boy, and it was taken off him, and he needs it to defeat the Snow Queen."

"Really?" said Mr. Whittard, but Ophelia could tell he wasn't listening anymore. That was what happened to her father when he was with swords.

"Miss Kaminski's showing me more dresses and jewels today," said Alice. "She said I might even be able to have my portrait painted by the museum artist."

"Well, that will keep you out of trouble," said Mr. Whittard. "But, Ophelia, you are staying with me today. Absolutely no wandering off. I don't want a repeat of yesterday's performance."

"Daddy," said Ophelia. She had so much she needed to do. "Please. I promise I won't get into any trouble."

Mr. Whittard looked at his youngest daughter, with her pale face and her ragged braids and her smudgy glasses. How much trouble could she possibly cause?

"No," said Mr. Whittard. "You're staying with me, and that is that."

It was terrible news. She had a fresh tin of sardines in front of her, and now she couldn't eat them. She slipped the unopened tin into her pocket, crossed her arms, and ignored everybody.

The best thing that can possibly be done in terrible situations is to look for the facts. That was Ophelia's maxim. As she walked through the frozen streets with her father and Alice, she organized the facts.

The facts were:

1. Boy locked in room 303;
2. Need chance to get to him and let him out;
3. Boy needs his magical sword;
4. Need to find the One Other, who is the only one who can use it to defeat the Snow Queen.

She wondered if boys from elsewhere were *Homo sapiens*. And wizards too. What family did they belong to? And what about Snow Queens? Where did they come from, and how did they reproduce? Was there a classification of magical things just as there was a classification of living things? Just asking these questions made her feel better.

"What on earth are you mumbling about?" asked Alice.

"None of your business," said Ophelia.

But to find the sword? She needed data, and she needed a grid to conduct her search. They walked across the square, past the giant Christmas tree and the ice-skating rink. She took the museum map from her pocket. Her plan was to take the map and shade in every room where there was a chance of a sword. Of course, her first stop would be *Battle: The Greatest Exhibition of Swords in the History of the World*. She would be able to look there while she was with her father But she could also try *Napoleonic Wars, Colonial Expansion, Chinese Empires, Egyptian Artifacts 3000–2000 BC*. There were also *Life on the Frontier, Men's Clothing Through Time, Japanese Ceremonial Dress*, and *History of the Incas*.

She knew her father would grow tired of his plan to keep her with him. He'd be too busy. All she needed to do was ask too many questions. When she had her chance, and she knew she would have one, she would race to the boy's room and release him, and together they could search these rooms.

When they arrived in the foyer, they unwound their scarves. Ophelia saw a huge sign had been erected. It said:

2 DAYS
~ UNTIL ~
The Wintertide Clock Chimes

It made Ophelia's stomach sink. Her stomach sank exactly the way it did when it was Lucy Coutts's turn to pick the medicine-ball teams.

They walked across the great, glittering wedding mosaic floor, and their footsteps echoed.

"What are you looking so worried about, O?" asked her father, turning back to her and taking her gently by the shoulders.

"Nothing," said Ophelia. How could she possibly tell him?

"Aren't you enjoying the holiday?" he asked, but before Ophelia could answer, he continued. "Just think, you and Alice could go to the winter markets this afternoon. Maybe you could find a small Christmas tree. I know how hard things have been, but we have to make the most of our time here."

That was as close as her father ever came to mentioning their mother. He could not, would not, speak her name or mention their sadness.

"You could go ice-skating again," he said.

"I guess," said Ophelia.

"Remember, portrait painting," said Alice, pointing to her face.

In the sword workroom Alice assumed her position on the old throne, looking very bored, while Ophelia sat beside her father at his worktable. She picked a light blue pencil and began to shade her map.

"What are you up to, then, Ophelia?" her father asked.

"I'm devising a plan for a large-scale search for that ancient and magical sword."

"Well, you'll have to stop your games for a moment, because we have to go to the sword exhibition hall now," said Mr. Whittard. "I'm going to do some work on the conquistadors."

"Good," said Ophelia. "That's exactly where I need to go."

The sword exhibition hall was on the main floor and bitterly cold. Exactly the same stinging cold as on the seventh floor and the sixth floor.

"Why is there no heating?" said Ophelia.

"I know, I know," muttered her father. "I tried to discuss it with Miss Kaminski yesterday but didn't get very far."

Their breaths billowed in front of them. In the exhibition hall the windows were covered in heavy velvet curtains, and all the lights were turned down low. The exhibition mannequins were covered in white sheets of plastic. There were hundreds of them. All standing in their places, from "Iron Age" to "Bayonets of World War I." She could see the outlines of them. They were all holding swords.

"A little creepy, isn't it, O?" said Mr. Whittard.

"Mummy would have liked it," whispered Ophelia.

"Yes," said Mr. Whittard. He wouldn't look at Ophelia. "Yes, she would have."

He finished what he was doing and ruffled Ophelia's bangs as he passed. He would change the subject now. She knew it. It was what he always did. He couldn't talk about it at all.

"Come on, then, work to be done," he said.

There were swords in glass cabinets, swords hanging in glinting lines on the walls, swords on pallets ready to be unloaded. There was a raised dais, and a large empty glass case stood in the middle of the room.

"Now, *that* is where Miss Kaminski's pride and joy is going to go," said her father. "She really is being very mysterious about it."

Mr. Whittard went to work on the conquistadors, placing the information panel and fiddling with the interactive screen. Ophelia went to work searching for the magical sword. She started with "Bronze Age." She lifted up the plastic on the mannequins and examined the swords. They were nothing like the sword that had belonged to the boy.

She wished she had remembered her gloves. She was always forgetting her gloves nowadays. She stuck her freezing hands in her pockets and felt the map, the puffer, and the keys. The keys made her feel guilty and proud at the same time. It was very confusing.

She moved between the displays. The mannequins were dressed according to their era. There were cavemen and crusaders, gladiators and Gallic warriors. There were Knights Templar, Teutonic soldiers, samurai, and Saracens. She peeked beneath the plastic carefully and examined each sword. The mannequins' hands were very white and very real. If she raised the sheet high enough, she could catch a glimpse of their faces, half in shadow. Each had the same large, ice-blue, staring doll eyes.

"Be careful with them," said Mr. Whittard. "They're all in exact positions."

"I will be," said Ophelia.

"I've just forgotten some passwords for this computer here," said Mr. Whittard. "Will you be okay for ten minutes while I run back?"

"Yes," she said.

"I won't be long."

"I'm fine."

When he was gone, Ophelia checked "Iron Age," "Mesopotamians," "Egyptians," and "Syrians." She checked "Greeks" and "Spartans." She hurried through "Viking Sword Masters" and "Boer Wars." She walked quickly, casting her eyes over every sword in the tall glass cabinets. There were long swords, short swords, elaborate swords, and plain swords. There were shining swords and crumbling swords half eaten away by time. But there was none that looked like the boy's sword. All she had left to look at were "Medieval Knights" and "Conquistadors."

Without the small sounds of her father's tinkering, it was deathly, horribly silent.

"I'm all right, but . . . ," said Ophelia, and she took a squirt on her puffer.

She tried to think of boys' names beginning with *D* to take her mind off the silence. Darius, Donald, Damien. Dale, Derek, Daniel. Deon, Dalton, Dougal. Darren, David. Something about *David* felt right. The hairs on her arms prickled. She would have to say that name to the boy and see if he felt anything.

There were two medieval knights in the display, with a large stuffed white horse. She lifted the plastic on the first of the knights. She looked up at his face. She sprang backward, her heart beating so hard that it nearly leapt out her chest.

"Don't be stupid," said Ophelia. "That knight did not just blink."

She took a step back toward the display. She lifted the plastic again to be sure. She made herself stare at the mannequin. The knight's eyelids didn't move at all. He was a perfectly normal mannequin. She lowered the sheet and tried to control her breathing.

She checked the next knight, and he was also perfectly normal. Just a perfectly normal, unblinking mannequin.

"Good," Ophelia said aloud at exactly the same time something touched her on the shoulder.

When she turned, there was nothing there. Nothing at all. Except the first knight who had blinked was standing in a different position—she was sure of it. Before, he had been facing the other way. What was that noise? She spun around. She had heard plastic rustling.

She moved into the center of the room, onto the raised dais, away from all the mannequins, her legs quivering. She knew she should run, but fear had sucked the air from her lungs. She wished her father would come back. Surely he would be back soon. She made a small squeaking sound.

She tried to think of what she should do.

Think, Ophelia, she thought. Think.

She thought of her mother's horror books and how there were always things creeping up behind the heroes or heroines. What if my mother were writing this scene right now? she thought. What if I were the heroine? What would she have me do?

She decided very quickly what it would be. She decided to shout very loud.

Ophelia shouted, "I am not afraid of you!"

She shouted it as loud as she could. Her voice reverberated in the still room.

"I am not afraid of you," Ophelia whispered this time. She turned in a full circle, pointing at all the displays. "So you can stop it. Stop it right now. Anything you might do is all in my imagination."

She marched up to the Spanish conquistadors and lifted up the plastic. They were nothing but mannequins holding on to swords. As soon as her back was turned, she heard the rustling of plastic again.

She had one more mannequin to look at, and she would be finished. She lifted the last piece of plastic. A Spanish conquistador was holding a very shiny silver cutlass. She looked up at his face just to make sure. The conquistador had a long, flowing black mustache but the same doll eyes as the rest. She was looking at his eyes when he grabbed her arm.

"Oh," said Ophelia, and she tried to wrench herself free.

The conquistador gripped her arm so tightly that she could not break away.

"Ouch," said Ophelia.

All around her was the terrible sound of plastic rustling.

"Please let me go!" she shouted as loud as she could.

The conquistador did not listen to her. She tried to prize his fingers from her arm.

"Please," she whispered as he began to lift her from the ground. "Daddy," she screamed. "Daddy!"

She heard the door to the exhibition hall being opened, and with that sound, she was released. She fell to the ground with a thump. Footsteps rushed toward her—high heels, the sharp sound of Miss Kaminski's high heels.

"Adelia," said Miss Kaminski. "What has happened?"

She knelt down beside Ophelia. Ophelia was enveloped in a soothing cloud of warm, sweet perfume.

"There, there," said Miss Kaminski. "Have you had a fright?"

"I . . . ," Ophelia began, pointing at the Spanish conquistador. "He . . ."

The conquistador had gone back to being just a mannequin covered in plastic.

"Now, now," said Miss Kaminski, with very kind eyes. "Don't speak."

Ophelia heard more feet, then saw her father's concerned face looking down at her. "I heard shouting," he said. "What happened?"

"There was . . . ," started Ophelia.

"Hush," said Miss Kaminski, and she put her finger to her perfectly painted lips. "She has a very big imagination. She should not be left alone in such a room." The museum curator helped Ophelia to her feet. "I will take her to the cafeteria, and she will have hot chocolate, Mr. Whittard. And I will show her the collection of dollhouses. There are too many swords in this room for a young girl."

When they were outside the sword exhibition hall, a little of the kindness drained out of Miss Kaminski's voice. "That is no place for a little girl," she said. "You won't go there again, will you?"

Miss Kaminski's hand, on Ophelia's cheek, was very cold.

"N-n-never again," stammered Ophelia.

* * *

The hot chocolate was good. Miss Kaminski watched Ophelia drink it, and her bright blue eyes sparkled. Ophelia didn't know which way to look or what to say; Miss Kaminski frightened her so. One minute kind, the next pinching her through her blue velvet coat. When Ophelia was finished, she took the museum curator's hand reluctantly and followed her into an elevator. She was duly deposited in the *Gallery of Dollhouses*.

"I am going to see your charming sister now," said Miss Kaminski. "Today I will have her portrait painted. What do you think of that, then, Nadia?"

"Ophelia," said Ophelia.

"If you become bored, you must go straight down in the elevator to your father's workroom. Nowhere else. But you will be here some time, I imagine. All little girls love dolls."

"Yes," said Ophelia. Even though she hated them. Even though she would have much rather looked at a fossil.

She didn't like Miss Kaminski. She didn't like her at all. Even if her perfume was nice, even if she looked like a fashion model. When she was near Miss Kaminski, she felt terrible and couldn't breathe, and as soon as she was gone, she took a squirt on her puffer.

The guard watched her carefully after the museum curator left and showed no sign of going to sleep. Ophelia approached her and asked where the nearest toilets were. The guard laughed a toothless laugh and pulled a map from her large black handbag. She pointed to where the nearest restrooms were.

Out in the corridor Ophelia heard her mother whisper in her ear.

Will you help him? she said. *Will you turn your back on him? Will you walk away and pretend he was never there at all?*

"Shh," said Ophelia.

You must help him, said her mother.

"I know," said Ophelia. And she began to run.

7

In which Ophelia meets a misery bird

———◆———

Ophelia pressed her eye to the keyhole, and there was the blue-green eye surrounded by dark lashes.

"I knew you'd come," the boy said.

"I got the second key," Ophelia said. "It was terrible. There were ghosts, horrible ghosts, in the loneliest place I've ever been. But one helped me. The bravest girl I've ever met."

"Braver than you?" asked the boy, incredulous.

"Far braver," said Ophelia. "And you didn't tell me about the snow leopards. Look, one scratched my arm with its claw just as the elevator doors were closing, and it hasn't stopped aching since."

"Have you cleaned the wound? You must clean the wound. All sorts of things can happen with magical wounds."

He held up his hand to the keyhole. Ophelia saw that his middle finger was missing. There was an ugly scar left behind. She looked quickly away.

"And just now I've been to the sword exhibition hall, because

I was sure that the sword would be there. So many swords are there, but not yours. A conquistador grabbed me but then let me go when Miss Kaminski came."

Ophelia took the plain old key from her pocket and held it in the palm of her hand. She knew it wouldn't open the door. She had known it even before she entered the room. It was such a small key.

"I'm sorry," said the boy. "You've been so brave, but now is the greatest challenge you'll face."

"You'd better not say the sixth or seventh floor," said Ophelia.

So the boy didn't say anything. Ophelia watched his eye watching the floor.

"Which?"

"The seventh. Room 707. I have been told by Mrs. V. and Mr. Pushkinova both. You must go soon, for the misery birds have just been fed and they'll be drowsy."

Ophelia looked at the windows, where the snow was falling and covering everything, all the rooftops and the cars in the streets and the spires of the great cathedrals and the small churches.

"I don't know if I can."

The seventh floor was so terrifying, even if there was nothing to see. Even though there were only doors.

"What if the Snow Queen comes?"

"I will teach you how to sense if she is coming," said the boy. "It's very simple and something you will need to know. Close your eyes."

Ophelia, kneeling beside the door, closed her eyes reluctantly.

"First you must forget almost everything, and instead concentrate on the weather," said the boy.

She opened her eyes and sighed.

"Close your eyes," said the boy. "There is a certain sort of chill that comes before the Queen. It is a bit like the cool that rises up from the grass in the morning just after dawn breaks. Do you know this chill?"

"I suppose," said Ophelia.

"Or perhaps the sudden drop in temperature just before snow. That cold that is almost like a metal, gray and frozen. Do you know this sensation?"

"I guess."

It was the boy's turn to sigh now. "Let's try your ears," he said. "Do you know the sound of snow falling through trees? It is a falling, sighing, lonely sort of sound."

Ophelia shrugged.

"Or perhaps your nose," said the boy. "She has two types of smell."

"Like what?"

"First, when she is nearby, her smell is very empty. It's like empty land, big sky, snow, and maybe a little bit like pinecones. Up close she is almost completely like . . . hot chocolate."

"I know the smell of hot chocolate," said Ophelia.

"That is usually the last thing you smell of her," said the boy. "When she is right near you."

"When it's too late," guessed Ophelia.

"When it's too late."

"Did the wizards teach you this?"

"Yes," said the boy. "This was one of the things the wizards taught me."

"What did they look like, those wizards?" she asked, and she couldn't believe she was asking such a thing.

She imagined the other children at the Children's Science Society of Greater London and what they'd think if she even mentioned wizards. Max Lowenstein, the cat expert, for instance. He wouldn't even try to be kind. He'd say, "Ophelia. Magic is not real. It is the misguided belief that you can somehow alter physical events through supernatural or mysterious means. If you believe in such a thing, you probably shouldn't come here again."

"Well, as I've said, they were very tall and very kind," said the boy, "except for Petal, who was short and plump. She was the one who made all their biscuits."

"Biscuits," said Ophelia, laughing, and she was going to ask what sort, but she noticed a look of terror in the boy's blue-green eye.

"Quickly," he said. "You must hide behind the curtain. I hear Mr. Pushkinova coming."

"I don't hear anything," she said.

"Trust me," said the boy. "Hide behind the curtains."

Ophelia stood up. There was not a single sound. She was sure of it. But she did as the boy asked and slipped behind the dusty velvet window curtains. No sooner was she there than she heard keys jangling.

"Hello, my Marvelous Boy," came an old man's voice. "Shall I take away your morning tray?"

"Yes, please, Mr. Pushkinova," said the boy. "How were the Queen's birds this morning?"

"Oh, they were hungry as normal," the old man replied. "And by tomorrow night they will be ravenous, of course, as they will not be fed again now until they are let free."

The boy said something, but Ophelia could not catch it. She heard Mr. Pushkinova sigh.

"Now, now, my Marvelous Boy, you know I cannot do that. I am your keeper and you are my prisoner, and that is how it has always been for these last seventy-nine years."

Ophelia heard the door being locked again.

"I will be back on the hour with your lunch," the old man said.

When she was sure he had gone, Ophelia slid from behind the curtain and knelt before the door.

"What does he mean, the birds shall be freed?" she whispered.

"He means they will be set free when the clock chimes and the ending begins."

"What will they do?"

"They will cause great misery," said the boy. "They will eat . . . people."

That left Ophelia unable to speak for some time.

"Maybe . . . ," she said finally, and then she stopped herself. Just the thought of the seventh floor made her weak at the knees.

"What?"

"Maybe I could find a way to stop their doors," she said.

"Some kind of sticky tar?" asked the boy.

That made Ophelia laugh. It was the high, nervous laugh of someone who is thinking of people-eating birds and trying not to.

"Superglue, perhaps," she said.

"I don't know this substance," said the boy. "But it sounds very strong."

"Is there a misery bird in 707?"

The boy didn't answer. Not at first. Ophelia pressed her ear against the keyhole, waited for his reply. She couldn't bear to look at his eye.

"If anyone can do it, I know it will be you," said the boy at last.

Which Ophelia took to mean yes. She took a squirt on her puffer. She would do it. She would do it, and that would be it. The boy would be free then, and he would able to look for the sword himself. He would be better at that. He knew, after all, what he was looking for.

She put the key back in her left-hand pocket with the other. She was still reluctant to go. She took off her glasses and cleaned them with her coat hem so that she could slow her breathing. She was scared. Couldn't the boy see it? He waited, not speaking.

"Tell me a bit more," she pleaded. She needed time to be braver, even just a little time. "Before I go. What happened with those owls that were chasing you?"

There were only three great magical owls. The wizards told me that. Then they told me what to do if I should meet one, but I wasn't listening. There was a cloud, you see, in the shape of a bear, floating past the window and I watched it pass, and by the time it was gone, the advice had been given and I'd missed it.

There are Ibrom and Abram and Alder. I have learned that since, from Mr. Pushkinova, who not only keeps the keys but knows everything there is to know about the Queen's army. He sometimes comes in the night and speaks through the keyhole, when he cannot sleep for his rheumatism, and he tells me such things.

Ibrom was the most magical of all, it is said. There are many minor magical owls, nearly always haunting houses and hospitals where people are about to die, but they are of no consequence, you see. When the spell coating me washed away with my tears, Ibrom smelt me. If it had been Alder or Abram, who are less magical but much more vicious, then perhaps I wouldn't be here today.

The strangest thing I have learned is that it's impossible to know what's inside someone. The wizards didn't teach me this, but I have learned it myself. Those who appear tall and straight and very good are sometimes rotten on the inside, and others, huge and clawed and apparently very bad, sometimes contain a pure and sweet form of goodness. The biggest trap is to judge a person by their outer casing. Their skin. Their hair. Their snow-white feathers.

Have you ever read about the great magical owls? Are they in your science books? Probably not. They are misunderstood and are horribly dangerous but also terribly sad. It is their sadness that gives them their magic. They find and keep the sorrows for the Queen. And the Queen needs the sorrows to exist. She needs them the way that others need air.

You see, Ibrom could hear someone crying in another land if he so chose. A boy, say, lost in a city or a woman wailing for that same child. He could sense all these things from high above. He could smell tears.

A great magical owl lives for many centuries, and Ibrom had lived for several. His magic allowed him to move freely between worlds and times. He had been witness to many sufferings: the sinkings of ships, swords, tanks, machine guns, torture, bombs, infernos, massacres. Untimely deaths, countless separations, endless grief. All these sufferings Ibrom related to the Snow Queen. They were recorded in ink on white paper. All the great tragedies and all the small tragedies, in columns neatly and exactly measured, town after town, city after city, hour after hour, day after day, year after year.

They were cross-referenced. Cataloged. Filed away. Kept.

And they are the Queen's proof that the world is terrible, and they are her proof that all her arguments are right. That everything should remain frozen and that death should reign supreme. Each day she walks in her library and touches these memories, and they make her stronger.

And she likes above all to destroy good things, delicate

morsels of innocence, which she puts in her machine. She extracts their souls and drinks the ruin of them in a cup. It was the three great magical owls who hunted her these things.

That day, when I left the kingdom, Ibrom was circling high in the sky. He could smell the huge cloud of fear that rose above the crowd on the road, grief too—the grief of hasty goodbyes—but this was not what he was looking for. He turned sharply, again and again, searching for me.

And there I was below, crying over hard bread and cheese.

There were great spikes of sadness rising up into the sky.

He found me quite quickly, as you can imagine.

He looked down on me, crying like a baby, through the trees.

I didn't know he was there. I had moved on in my thinking and was now lamenting the fact that I had forgotten which tree I was meant to use for making a strengthening tea. And there I was expected to remember many things and carry a magical sword, and I couldn't even remember the simplest of things. It made me cry all the more. Ibrom circled just above the forest canopy.

What could he see? Me untying my laces to examine my blisters. The crown of my hair, my brown face. He kept quiet, that great magical owl, until he could keep quiet no more. He let out one long screech and plummeted down through the trees.

I looked up and saw him. He was coming straight toward me. He was as large as me, maybe larger, his wings—huge white, glittering sails—blotting out my vision. I rolled to the side and he barely missed me.

Now, what was it that the wizards had told me about the owls? There was something I was supposed to remember. If only I had listened to that lesson. The owl swooped steeply back up through the trees to take his position. I felt for the sword, dragged it from its scabbard, but it immediately nosed to the ground. It was so heavy, my hands shook just trying to hold the thing. And already Ibrom was descending and screeching again.

This time I somersaulted beneath him, and he held my ankle briefly in his great talons. I rose in the air with him before twisting free. The owl shot upward again toward the trees.

I pulled the one arrow from my quiver—yes, one arrow, another fact to lament—and drew my bow.

I stood the way the wizards had taught me. Felt the earth through my bare feet. I wished more than anything that the wizards had taught me something magical. Now I was going to be eaten by an owl and I was only a short way from the town.

Earth, bare feet. If you ever have to shoot a great magical owl with an arrow, you should remember this, Ophelia. Everything is connected. If you touch the ground, you touch the tops of the trees. If you touch the trees, you touch the wings of birds.

The arrow thrummed free from my bow. It flew straight and true, upward, upward, upward until it lodged in Ibrom's breast. The great magical owl fell to the ground with a thump. The forest floor shook, the leaves whispered, a curious stillness descended.

Does it seem too simple to you? I was so shocked that he fell that way, my arrow through his heart. How could it be? Ibrom lay on his side, lifting one wing helplessly. I went toward him. What was it they had told me about magical owls? Was it that I was never, under any circumstances, meant to kill them? But the wizards *had* taught me to always assist those in need.

The owl stared at me. He was not dead, only terribly injured. Looking into his eyes, Ophelia, I felt like I was looking into a flame.

"I'm so sorry," I said. Then I remembered. "I mean, hello. I mean, I come in friendship and mean you no harm."

Which seemed an awful thing to say, considering what I'd just done.

"I am a boy chosen by a protectorate of wizards from the east, west, and middle to deliver this sword so that the Snow Queen may be defeated."

Ibrom closed his fiery eyes and opened them again. "Yes, yes, yes, I know all this," he whispered. Flinched. Raised his great wing.

"What should I do?" I asked. "Should I take the arrow from you?"

"No," said Ibrom. The owl's voice was so deep, the forest trembled beneath my feet. "Come closer, so I can see you."

I crawled forward. Ibrom lifted his huge feathered head, but it fell back again.

"Much is spoken of you," said the owl. "How you have been sent to save the world. You are small. Smaller than I imagined. But you smell delicious. If I had caught you, I would have taken you by the shirt so as not to mark your skin. I would have taken you to my nest and gazed at you all night before educating you in the ways of misery."

Which are terrible words, are they not? But I could tell he was not all bad.

"You see, I can look forward in time just as well as your wizards can," he continued. "And I have seen the One Other, who is just as small and just as puny. I have spent nights beside her bedroom, looking upon her. I know that she will never be of use to anyone, not against the Queen. Not against snow and sadness.

"The hopelessness of it—two such beings entrusted to save all the realms. None of it is possible."

"What would give you comfort?" I asked. "I shouldn't have shot that arrow. It's just that you were going to—"

"I travel the world," Ibrom interrupted. Even his whisper made my body shake. "I have seen great, unthinking machines made by men to perform horrible deeds. I have seen guns as huge as elephants and bombs that have laid waste to whole cities. I have seen battlefields where dying men are eaten by crows. I have seen immeasurable sorrows. The Queen desires you, and it was my task to find you and take you to her."

I looked into his unearthly eyes.

Ibrom gazed back. His body vibrated with unused magic. "Come closer," he said. "I have a proposition for you. If you will give me a small part of yourself, I will give you a portion of myself in return. This exchange will provide you with a charm. This magical blessing will keep you safe from the Queen for just a little while, long enough for you to make it to the valley forest, where the wolves will not follow you. The Queen will be unable to harm you in this time, and if she does, she will harm the whole of her army. So tightly are we bound together by her misery."

What should I do? Should I believe such a creature? What would you do, Ophelia, in such a situation? The owl closed his eyes and waited. Is that what the wizards had taught me? Never, under any circumstances, trust a dying owl?

"Which part will I give you?" I asked.

"A finger, perhaps?"

"Will it hurt?"

"Only for a while."

So I looked at my fingers for a long time while the owl took terrible, shuddering breaths. I wished I could make decisions. The world was so full of things I had to decide. If I made the wrong decision, everything would be wrong. Everything. And it wasn't fair again, you see. I needed my fingers. I needed them to hold sticks, and to fish, and to pick up stones from the river and skip them across the bright morning water. I thought of all these things; then I held out my hand to the owl.

"Shush," said Ophelia. She held her own hand, protecting her fingers against nothing. "Don't tell me any more."

"Mr. Pushkinova will be back with my lunch soon anyway,"

said the boy. "What about the third key? That's what is important now. We don't have much time. And this magical tar you speak of?"

"It's superglue," said Ophelia. "And it's not really magical. I'll go now."

"Be careful," said the boy.

Which is all very well to say, thought Ophelia, when you have to enter a room containing a magical beast that likes to eat people. "I'll be back soon," she said.

She raced to the sword workroom, where Mr. Whittard was holding a rusted rapier in his hands. He was looking at it as though he were holding the greatest of treasures. Sometimes he had looked at Ophelia's mother in this way. When Susan returned from a walk, for instance, and her cheeks were pink and her hair wet with rain and she was so full of stories that she glowed.

Ophelia waited patiently beside her father until he stopped looking at the sword and noticed her.

"There you are," said Mr. Whittard. "Are you feeling better? How were the dolls? It was very nice of Miss Kaminski to organize all that. She really is very kind."

Ophelia didn't like the way he said *Miss Kaminski*. He said *Miss Kaminski* as though he were thinking of something special. And he knew Ophelia certainly didn't like dolls.

"I'm feeling much better, thank you," she said. "But I need some superglue."

"Whatever for?"

"Well, it's a surprise, really."

"I don't like the sound of that."

"Please, Daddy. I promise it's for nothing bad. I'm meeting Alice," she lied. "She's having her picture painted, remember? And the superglue . . . is for something I'm working on. Miss Kaminski is letting me fix some of the old doll furniture while I watch. She said I looked like the kind of girl who could help with such a job. I'll be gone for ages. Portraits take a long time, you know."

"Well, in that case," said her father. He looked around, then opened and shut a few drawers. "There were a few huge tubes here, actually."

Finally he located a drawer containing several large yellow tubes with extra-long nozzles.

Ophelia was surprised by how easily she lied. She had two stolen keys in her pockets, and the lies were sliding off her tongue. Soon she'd probably be shoplifting. She expected that was how it started.

At the foot of the staircase, she turned to her father. "You haven't seen that sword, have you?" she asked. "The one with the wooden handle and the closed eye? The magical one?"

"No, but if I find it, I will tell you," said Mr. Whittard, and calling after her, added, "Wait, we're having dinner tonight with Miss Kaminski, so I'll need you and Alice back here by five o'clock sharp. Alice has promised me she'll take you to buy a dress."

Dresses, thought Ophelia as she raced up the stairs. She couldn't remember the last time she'd worn a dress. She certainly didn't own one. Why on earth was her father trying to get her to wear a dress? Her mother would never have tried. Her mother would have said, "I hope you didn't take those jeans out of the dirty clothes basket?" And if Ophelia had, she would have shaken her head and said, "There is no hope for you, O. Really, there is no hope."

Ophelia stopped walking and closed her eyes. This happened sometimes when she thought of her mother. She felt she couldn't move, not another step; couldn't take another breath. That must have been what it felt like for the boy, when he thought about the bread and cheese. She could almost sit down on the stairs and begin to cry. But she didn't.

Instead she started ascending the stairwell again slowly. She tapped her left-hand pocket. She felt the two keys there, her puffer, the museum map, the tin of sardines. She looked down at the tube of superglue in her hand. She inhaled a deep breath of the fusty museum air, steeling herself for what she had to do.

In the dinosaur hall Ophelia slipped the superglue inside her coat. She looked at the elevator with the large cross on the doors and shuddered. She pretended to look at some dinosaur knee bones. The old guard watched her every move and took almost twenty minutes of furious knitting to fall asleep.

Ophelia walked past the elevator three times until she worked up the courage to enter it. She touched the superglue inside her coat. She had expected magic to be very clean and powerful, but instead it was messy and uncomfortable and full of decisions. It made her legs tremble.

Ophelia pressed the number 7.

* * *

The seventh floor was just as quiet and cold and still as it had been on her last visit. The elevator doors opened loudly, making her wince. She stepped into the silence. Her skinny knock-knees shook inside her too-big jeans; each breath caught in her throat. She reached into her pocket and very carefully took the plain key she had stolen from the box in the snow leopard room. She scratched a little at the greenish color with her fingernail and saw, engraved in small writing on its side, the number 707. She placed it back in her pocket.

In the left corridor she moved as noiselessly as she could, her heart beating in her ears. She took the superglue and unscrewed the top, and at door number 701 she inserted the nozzle in the keyhole and squeezed. She was careful with the drops. She moved to number 702 and then number 703, squeezing in the clear liquid.

When her breathing slowed and her heartbeat quieted, she could hear again. There were soft sighing sounds coming from behind the doors. She tried not to think of them. She tried not to think of the other rustlings that had now become apparent. She tried not to think of the very strong feathery smell. She glued up the locks of 704 through 714, skipping number 707. She glued up the locks of 715 through 721. She heard the clank of the elevator doors closing and the elevator going away to another floor.

Which meant that someone had called it.

Which made her freeze, with the superglue in her hands.

Maybe someone had called it and they were going to another floor, she thought. She turned the corner, where the remaining doors were, and also the little white cupboard, from which she had stolen the first key. She quickly glued up locks 722 to 730. Then she did the same for 731, 732, 733, and 734.

She was back in the first corridor when she heard the whir of the elevator motor. The elevator was returning. She wished suddenly, more than anything, that she had never met the boy behind the door—it didn't matter how interesting or exciting he was, it didn't matter that he had been given lessons by wizards, which she shouldn't really believe in, or that he had been given a blessing by a great magical owl. She took the two steps she needed as the elevator doors began to open, fumbled with the key to 707, inserted and turned it. Then she stepped inside and closed the door softly behind her.

The misery bird was five times her size and hanging upside down, fast asleep. She dared not breathe. It was just as the boy had said, the ugliest, most horrible thing she had ever seen. The bird had the head of a fierce eagle, tucked tenderly into the snow-white plumage of its chest. It had the black leathery wings of a giant bat, folded neatly at its sides. Its terrifying talons gripped a bar that ran across the ceiling. Each time it exhaled slowly, the wind from its silvery beak ruffled Ophelia's hair.

Ophelia could not take her eyes from it.

It's a monster. It's a monster. It's a monster, her head said.

The bird monster slept.

She heard footsteps in the corridor. The sound of high heels clipping on the marble. Ophelia was suddenly so cold that she could not stop herself from trembling, and her teeth began to rattle in her mouth. It must be the Queen. A phone rang. The footsteps stopped suddenly, and Ophelia heard someone sigh.

"What?" a woman's voice said. "Can you handle nothing alone? Must I do everything?"

The footsteps receded.

It must have been the Queen. Did Snow Queens use phones? It must have been.

Ophelia stood before the misery bird, trying to think of what to do. She heard the elevator doors open and shut and the elevator clank away to a lower floor. Everything would be all right. She would find the key. There in the corner of the room was a golden box. Only that golden box could contain the golden key that would work in the golden keyhole. She would open that box and take out the key. She would open the door and then glue it shut. She'd go to the elevator and press DOWN and tell the boy that she couldn't possibly help anymore. Yes, that was exactly what she'd do. She took one step toward the box, as quietly as she could.

The misery bird opened its wings.

The misery bird's wings opened so suddenly and with such a snap that it made Ophelia fall backward and land with a bump on the ground. Its wings snapped open like a deathly black fan and trembled slightly. They almost filled the room. The bird opened its luminous gray eyes. It made a dangerous, low noise in its throat.

"I'm sorry," whispered Ophelia. "I didn't mean to wake you."

The bird peered at her.

Now she was going to be eaten. She knew it. It wasn't fair. Her father would always wonder what had happened to her. He would say, "She went somewhere with superglue and then we never saw her again."

Ophelia closed her eyes and waited for the end.

She waited and waited, and then she got tired of waiting and opened her eyes.

The bird was staring at her with its intelligent eyes. It stretched its long, thin neck out and came very close to her face. It sniffed her features slowly. Its breath made Ophelia close her eyes again. She made a little squeak. She couldn't help it. The bird sniffed her hair and sniffed her shoulders and sniffed her pockets. First her right, then her left.

It took her left pocket within its powerful beak and ripped it clean off. The map, the sardines, the puffer, and the keys clattered to the ground. The bird stretched its neck all the way down and examined these things. Finally it took the sardine tin and brought it up to Ophelia.

She took it with shaking hands. She pulled the ring top and peeled the lid open.

"Is this what you want?" she croaked.

The bird opened its massive beak. She picked a sardine out and placed it on its hard gray tongue. When it had swallowed, it opened its mouth again. While she fed the bird, she knelt down and picked up the keys. She took a tiny step sideways toward the little box on the floor in the corner of the room. Then another. The bird's neck stretched after her and the sardines.

"Nice birdie," she said, plucking another sardine and placing it on its tongue.

She knelt down again, picked up the golden box from the ground, and placed another sardine in the misery bird's mouth. She took the key and opened the lock, a task that required her to hold the sardine tin and the key together in one hand. A task that required her to remove her eyes from the misery bird's face. She felt its breath on her neck. She squeaked. She fumbled inside the box for the key. There it was. It was a long golden key, exactly the right size for the boy's prison door.

"More," she said to the misery bird. "Have some more."

She placed the last sardine from the tin in the bird monster's mouth.

"Can I go now?" whispered Ophelia.

Trembling, she picked up her puffer and map and glue. The misery bird looked at her closely. It yawned with its sardine breath. It retracted its neck and tucked its head neatly under its wing. Ophelia thought that probably meant yes. She walked to the door, her legs like wobbly stilts.

She opened the door very carefully.

The bird watched her with one eye.

She closed it. She inserted the superglue nozzle in the keyhole and squeezed. She moved back along the corridor to the large empty room and the elevator. She would let the boy out, she thought, and then that was it. He was on his own. She pressed the elevator button and heard it approaching from below. If the Queen was in the elevator, it would be the end of her. She knew it. She felt quite suddenly as though she was going to wet her pants. Up, up, up the elevator came. The doors slid open. It was empty. Ophelia pushed the button marked DOWN and sank to the floor inside.

She was a girl without coat pockets. She stuffed the three keys in her jeans and ran with the map and puffer and the remains of the glue in her hands, throwing the sardine tin into a receptacle as she went. She wasn't so sure about the Queen's machine; the misery birds were probably the real reason children went missing in the museum.

It was late, the sun starting to sink behind the city and the great Christmas tree. On the streets the pale children, in their silvery puffy coats, were already arriving with their skates in their hands, to circle round and round the ice rink, with their frozen faces and their empty eyes. Her father would be waiting for her. Perhaps he already knew she'd lied. He'd probably ban her from coming to the museum ever again.

She ran past the *Triceratops* and the *Tyrannosaurus rex*—the guard now gone—and she ran along the darkening corridors. She ran upstairs and downstairs and in and out of the great glittering galleries until she found the small lonely room of teaspoons. She raced down the gloomy gallery of painted girls, across the celebrated sea monster mosaic, and into the room of broken stone angels. She collided with Mr. Pushkinova, the map, puffer, and superglue falling to the floor. The tall old man held her arms to stop her from falling too. His hands were grayish and cool.

"I'm so sorry," said Ophelia. "I didn't see you there."

"What are you doing here?" asked Mr. Pushkinova very slowly and very quietly. She didn't know if he whispered or hissed the words.

"I was just . . ."

"What have you got here?" he asked. He reached down to the ground, and Ophelia heard his bones creaking. He took the superglue first and examined it, then her puffer and the map. He opened the map and looked at all her careful shading. He handed the items back to her.

"Interesting." He definitely hissed this time.

"It's just . . . ," said Ophelia.

But she didn't finish. Mr. Pushkinova leaned suddenly forward so that his face was inches from hers. Ophelia looked at his small, angry mouth and his ancient, stained teeth, which, when she was up close like that, looked a little too pointy. She looked into his terrible, cloudy eyes.

"I will warn you only once: do not meddle in magic, little girl," whispered Mr. Pushkinova. "There is nothing that you can do which will help the Marvelous Boy."

He took a deep breath. What was he going to do? Ophelia had a terrible sense that it wasn't something very nice. Then he did the not very nice thing.

He bared his teeth.

A vile, low growl rumbled from within him.

Ophelia turned and ran. She ran as fast as she could. She ran across the sea monster mosaic, down the gloomy gallery of painted girls, into a small, hushed circular library. She crouched beneath a spiral staircase. She hugged her arms around herself, shaking. She shook so violently that she thought her teeth were going to break apart. Then when she stopped shaking, she put her head in her hands and began to cry.

She sobbed until her sleeves were wet, because she had forgotten her handkerchief. She cried because she had no handkerchief. She cried because she didn't know what to do. If her mother had been there, *she* would have known what to do. *And* she would have had a handkerchief. She cried because Mr. Pushkinova was a horrible man. There was nothing good about him. How could the boy say there was anything good about him? It wasn't fair. It wasn't fair that she had been scratched by a snow leopard and pushed by ghosts and nearly eaten by a misery bird and growled at by a horrible man. She wasn't used to that sort of thing. And now she was going to be late again, and Alice would look at her missing coat pockets and raise her perfectly plucked eyebrows.

Then in the middle of feeling sad, she started to feel angry.

What did Mr. Pushkinova know?

How did he *know* she couldn't help the boy?

She wiped her eyes. He didn't know anything. He didn't know anything at all. If she wanted to rescue the boy and find the sword and save the world, then she could. And she would.

That's my girl, her mother whispered in her ear.

Ophelia pulled down on her braids hard until she felt better, and then she stood up and ran to meet Alice in the foyer.

8

*In which dinner is eaten in a revolving restaurant
and Ophelia falls asleep at a crucial moment*

———◆———

Ophelia stared at her reflection in the darkened hotel window. Alice had braided her hair so tight that Ophelia felt her brain wouldn't work. Her sister hadn't noticed her missing pockets at all. Alice's eyes were bright as diamonds. Humming a tuneless song, she stared right through Ophelia. Ophelia looked down at her stupid red dress with its stupid puffy sleeves and her stupid shiny black shoes.

If her mother had been alive, she would have said, "Stop worrying; you look lovely." She would have taken Ophelia's glasses and cleaned the smudges off them with the hem of her skirt. Ophelia would have looked at her, all blurred at the edges, and it would have been a very soothing thing.

Even when her mother became sick, she kept writing. Each morning when Ophelia was still in bed, she heard her mother's footsteps on the stairs, the study door opening, the sound of the computer turning on.

"You should be resting," she heard her father say one morning.

"But I have this idea," her mother replied.

"There is all the time in the world for ideas," her father said.

"Malcolm," her mother replied, so softly Ophelia barely heard it. "There isn't."

They were to meet Miss Kaminski on the highest floor of the hotel, in the revolving restaurant. Alice had spent over an hour applying makeup. Mr. Whittard was in a state. He had lacquered down his hair and dressed in his best black suit.

"Now, O," he said, smoothing down his tie. "You must be on your best behavior, and no nonsense about finding a magical sword."

"But I *do* have to find a magical sword," said Ophelia. "And I don't have very much time."

"That's exactly what I'm talking about," said her father.

He wanted to impress Miss Kaminski. Ophelia knew it in her bones. He had no idea how horrible Miss Kaminski was. He had no idea of how she looked so perfect but really was nothing but nasty.

"Ophelia can't be normal," said Alice, examining herself in her powder puff mirror. "It's impossible."

"Now, now, Alice, I haven't heard you say a single kind word to your sister since we arrived here," said Mr. Whittard. "All I'm saying is there will be important things to discuss tonight, and I want you both on your best behavior."

* * *

Miss Kaminski was fashionably late. She wore a silver dress beaded with crystals, and the skin of her arms was snow-white. She had let her hair out, and it shone in the candlelight. Miss Kaminski had the kind of beauty that stayed pressed against your eyes, like the halo you see after you look directly into the sun. Even when she stopped looking at Miss Kaminski and turned away, Ophelia felt her bright, nuclear glow. She took off her glasses and rubbed her eyes.

Mr. Whittard sat opposite Miss Kaminski, a vacant expression in his eyes, as though he had witnessed a miracle. It made Ophelia feel sad when she saw that. Not a crying sort of sad but a deep, aching sad that made her bones feel heavy. She felt cold. There was something wrong with the heating in the restaurant. She hugged herself, saw the gooseflesh on Alice's bare arms.

The restaurant rotated slowly. Ophelia felt its rumbling through her feet on the floor. The window showed the expanse of gray towers reaching out to the wharf, the frozen sea. All the gray streets, filled with people with their pale, exhausted faces. The old city came into view: the square; the skating rink almost empty of skaters; the huge, tinkling, sparkling Christmas tree.

The museum came next, sliding into view, its dark silhouette against the gray sky, the outlines of all the buttresses and gargoyles and stone men and stone lions. She thought of the boy there, all alone, waiting for her. She opened the little black purse Alice had made her take and looked at the three keys.

Miss Kaminski talked elegantly and charmingly about the

exhibition. "The world has never seen such an exhibition," she said. "And tomorrow the greatest sword of them all will arrive from the city vaults."

"I can't wait to see this sword," said Mr. Whittard. "You must tell me more of its strange history."

"Patience," said Miss Kaminski. She smiled conspiratorially at Mr. Whittard. "First I would like to ask Delia a question."

"Ophelia," said Ophelia.

"Yes," said Miss Kaminski, as though her name were an inconsequential matter. "Tell me, how did you find the exhibition of dolls this morning?"

"It was nice, but my favorite will always be the dinosaurs," said Ophelia. She needed to change the subject; she didn't want her father to find out she hadn't been with Miss Kaminski and Alice in the afternoon.

"But yes," said Miss Kaminski. "I've heard you are especially fond of the dinosaur hall. What other things have you found which amuse you?"

"You quite liked the history of Vikings, didn't you?" said Alice quickly.

"And you liked the static display of telephones," said Mr. Whittard.

"And the big room of fossils," said Alice. "You said you quite liked that."

"No, I didn't," said Ophelia. "What I'm really interested in is finding a—"

"What about that big clock?" said Alice. "You are always hanging around that room."

"It is a very important clock," said Miss Kaminski.

"It's counting down to the end of the world," said Ophelia.

The smile froze on Miss Kaminski's face. Ophelia had never noticed how white Miss Kaminski's teeth were. They shone.

Mr. Whittard brayed with laughter.

"Where do you get your ideas, child?" asked Miss Kaminski.

"Ophelia's mother was a famous horror writer," explained Mr. Whittard.

The curator's face unfroze. She flicked her white napkin out onto her lap and smiled so beautifully, Mr. Whittard fell back into his chair. "She has quite a remarkable imagination," she said, and she looked at Ophelia in a way that burnt.

For the rest of the dinner Miss Kaminski spoke of swords and the history of the museum.

"We have timed this exhibition, the greatest exhibition in the world, to coincide with the chiming of the Wintertide Clock," she said. "It will be such a wonderful night. People will be arriving from all four corners of the world. They will fill the galleries and fill the hallways and fill the city streets. And, Alice, I have a special task for you. I should like you to wear a special gown on Christmas Eve, a gown so special it is not on display. If you would like, you could hold the shears to cut the ribbon to open the evening."

"Really?" said Alice, holding her hand over her heart.

"And tomorrow we will hang your portrait," said Miss Kaminski, "if your father agrees. I know just the place."

Mr. Whittard beamed. The restaurant revolved. The museum came into view and disappeared again. Miss Kaminski looked at Alice and Mr. Whittard, but Ophelia sensed, more than anything, she was watching her. It was a terrible feeling. It made her unable to eat her pasta with sardines. She was shivering with the cold, and all the shivering was making her very tired.

"Your little one needs her bed," said Miss Kaminski.

It was a motherly type of thing to say. Mr. Whittard patted Ophelia on the head.

"Sleepy, sleepy little one," said Miss Kaminski, and just the way she sang that made Ophelia yawn and her eyes close. Miss Kaminski leaned forward and blew out the candle on the table, and the charm on her necklace became visible.

"That's gorgeous," said Alice. "Does it open something special?"

"That's my secret," said Miss Kaminski mysteriously.

Ophelia did not see or hear. Her father had scooped her up in his arms and was carrying her toward the elevator. She had fallen into the deepest of sleeps.

9

In which Ophelia visits the museum at night

———◆———

Ophelia was rushing through the museum. She was racing through the long, empty corridors in the dark, and something was close behind her. The thing close behind her was bad, very bad, and she ran as fast as she could. Her chest constricted, her legs ached. She willed herself not to turn, to see the thing following her. When she finally made it to the boy's room, she dropped to her knees and scrambled to the keyhole.

"Are you there?" she whispered.

There was no reply. She looked inside, but the room was empty. She was filled with such grief that it hurt her to breathe.

Then fear.

Fear freezing her.

She knew she must turn, because the thing was now in the room behind her. It was coming closer and closer and closer. She felt the hairs on her neck rise.

She moved upward out of her dream, surfacing, and found herself awake, taking gulps of midnight air. She stared at her watch. Only a few hours had passed since the restaurant. She stared at the dial, calculating: it was exactly three months, nine days, and half an hour since her mother had died.

"Daddy," she said, slipping out of bed. He was in the lounge working over a pile of spreadsheets.

"Hello, darling," he replied. "What are you doing awake again?"

"Can I sit with you?"

"You can for a minute," said Mr. Whittard, "but I'm actually heading back to the museum. I've got to tweak some things with the gladiators and prepare for the centerpiece sword that is arriving in the morning."

"Can I come with you?" She went over to him.

"No, of course you can't. You're exhausted. Look at you."

"I promise I'll just lie in that big throne," said Ophelia, "and sleep."

"I'll be in and out of the workroom all night. I'm afraid it's impossible," said Mr. Whittard. "I'm just too busy."

Ophelia took off her glasses and rubbed her eyes. She let her bottom lip tremble ever so slightly. If there was one thing she knew her father couldn't deal with, it was her crying.

"I don't feel like being alone," she said.

"Your sister's here," said her father, exasperated. Then he looked at Ophelia. "Oh goodness, now don't cry. Okay, then. But you'll have to bring a pillow and a blanket. And put on some warm clothes. There's absolutely no heating there at night."

Ophelia dressed quickly in her jeans and velvet coat, and

pulled a beanie down over her ears. She stuffed the three keys inside her denim pockets. She followed her father back to the museum, carrying a pillow and a blanket through the snow. Her ears burnt and her nose went numb. She was very glad when they made it to the museum and her father ran his key card over the side entrance door. The museum foyer was dim and cavernous and filled with the echoes of their footsteps. The wedding mosaic floor glimmered and sparkled in places in the half-light. Ophelia looked at the King, with his luxuriant dark hair, and the Queen, with the white locks spilling over her shoulders like a fountain.

When she looked up, she saw her father waiting for her, shaking his head.

"My girl, the dreamer," he said. "And the dawdler. Whatever happened to your pocket? It's hanging by a thread."

"It's a long story," said Ophelia.

She'd like to tell him, but she knew she couldn't. He probably wouldn't listen anyway. Or he'd start to listen, and then she'd see his eyes glass over and look past her at something she couldn't see.

In the sword workroom her father made her sit on the throne. She pretended to leaf through *Swords of the Ancient World*, Volume XIX. Miss Kaminski had arranged for two men to be there to help her father with the lifting and carrying, and Ophelia didn't have to wait long before her father left the room with them.

When he was gone, Ophelia put the pillow and the blanket on the throne in such a way that it looked like she was curled up sleeping. She placed her beanie, stuffed with tissue paper, at the top, then took her shoes and stuck the soles out at the very bottom. She was almost certain it would work. Her father would be engrossed in his preparations. He wouldn't exactly forget Ophelia, but he wouldn't exactly remember her either.

Sometimes, between her father and mother, she was surprised that she and Alice had survived at all. Her father was always thinking of fabulous swords and her mother had always been thinking about monsters and heroines.

She ran up the stairs into the dark museum. How different it was at night! And so cold. Shadows loomed and fell away as she passed. There were many strange noises: a curtain flapping, an elevator humming, the *clink clank* of work in the sword exhibition hall a long way off. Each noise she heard she imagined was Mr. Pushkinova, about to leap out of the shadows.

Ah! said her mother in her ear. *See how it feels to do dangerous things! I knew you'd come back. I knew you'd be brave.*

Ophelia smiled as she ran in her stocking feet. She ran through the *Gallery of Time*, filled with clocks, where the Wintertide Clock was tick, tick, ticking in the shadows. She peered into the gloom at the little gilt window and saw there was no longer a 2 but a 1. It gave her a falling feeling. It was just like the feeling she got when Lucy Coutts chose the medicine-ball teams and left Ophelia until the very end. Yes, that feeling, only one hundred times worse.

She ran through the room filled with teaspoons, the room filled with telephones, the room filled with mirrors. Her many reflections flickered beside her. She passed down the long hallway of painted girls in party dresses, pausing briefly in front of Kyra Marinova, who seemed to smile at her in the darkness. Up the stairs and down again, across the sea monster mosaic, through the gallery of broken angels, and into the boy's room.

"Are you there?" she whispered through the keyhole.

"Yes," he said. "I'm so glad you've come. I thought . . ."

She saw the glint of his bright eye, knew he too was filled with relief.

"I nearly got eaten by a misery bird," she said. "But it liked the sardines I had instead, and then Mr. Pushkinova caught me and growled at me and told me that I couldn't help you."

"Yes, he has been checking me more frequently," said the boy. "He wouldn't have meant to scare you so. Even though he is bad, he is really very good inside."

Ophelia didn't agree, but she didn't say so. She took the large golden key from her jeans pocket and held it in her palm. She placed it in the golden keyhole and opened the little door hidden in the turquoise sea.

· PART TWO ·

10

*In which the boy is released from
his prison after many years*

———◆———

They were bashful at first. The rescued and the rescuer. The boy stepped out of the room and looked out the window. He was not much taller than Ophelia. His bangs hung in his eyes. He brushed them away and smiled at her shyly. He wore very old-fashioned clothes: stockings and knickerbockers and shiny slippers. His fabulous coat was embroidered in gold, but it was very worn and tatty, and threads were unraveling at the sleeves. He plucked at one of these. Ophelia turned the key over and over in her hand.

"I didn't know if you would," said the boy.

"I didn't know either," said Ophelia.

"You're very brave," said the boy.

"I probably shouldn't do it again," she replied. "I have very bad asthma."

"We should begin to search for the sword."

"And then find you a hiding place," said Ophelia. "Maybe

we could just run away. I mean, out the front door. I could hide you in our hotel suite. There's this little dressing room. I could make you a bed in there until we work out what to do. If I told my father, he would listen eventually, if I told him enough."

"I've tried before," said the boy. "She always finds me. There are many spies in the city."

Ophelia looked out at the snow falling. When she looked at the boy from the corner of her eye, she was surprised to see how faded he seemed. His edges seemed indistinct, as though he were hardly there. Yet when she looked back at him, he was perfectly normal again. She thought she'd better not mention this to the boy.

"Let's start," she said.

"Yes," said the boy. "Let's start."

Ophelia and the boy tiptoed through *Mesopotamian Mysteries*, which contained a large papier-mâché ziggurat. They walked through *A Day in Roman Life*. They looked in the *Customs of Marriage*, *Religious Embroidery*, and *A Quaker Kitchen*. They picked their way through *History of Toys*. There were teddy bears and train sets and china dolls lined up to the ceiling, but there were no swords. They searched in *Taxidermy Treasures*, which was a vast hall filled with nothing but gloomy stuffed animals. Stuffed tigers and stuffed bison. Stuffed rabbits and stuffed lambs. Stuffed cats and stuffed dogs. It seemed there was nothing that had not been killed and frozen in time.

They went through *Napoleonic Wars*, *Colonial Expansion*, *Chinese Empires*, *Egyptian Artifacts 3000–2000 BC*, and *Life on the Frontier.* There were no magical swords. They visited *Men's Clothing Through Time, Japanese Ceremonial Dress,* and *History of the Incas.* No magical swords. Where swords had once been, there were only slips of paper, carefully typed: THIS SWORD IS ON LOAN TO BATTLE: THE GREATEST EXHIBITION OF SWORDS IN THE HISTORY OF THE WORLD (OPENING 6 P.M. SHARP CHRISTMAS EVE, WHEN THE WINTERTIDE CLOCK CHIMES).

They entered *Lives of Women in the Nineteenth Century* on a whim. There were commodes and potbelly stoves, fans, colorful clogs, hairbrushes, baby bonnets, and perambulators, but no magical swords.

"The problem is," said Ophelia, "that it's like looking for a needle in a haystack."

"It is hidden somewhere, I'm sure of it," said the boy.

Ophelia stopped walking.

"I can never, ever go to the seventh floor again," she said firmly. "And I've glued all the doors shut so we wouldn't be able to open them anyway. Also, what about this One Other? Maybe we should try to find him or her. Maybe he or she knows where the sword is."

It felt good to be organized.

"We need to find the sword first," said the boy. "Trust me."

"Trust me," he said again when Ophelia looked unsure. She pulled down on her braids hard.

"I've been trying to think of your name," she said as they began to walk again. "I thought if I said some names to you, one of them might mean something. You might feel something."

The boy smiled at her, uncertain.

"Here, let's try *E*," said Ophelia. "Ernest. Engelbert. Ebenezer. Edmund. Edgar. Feel anything?"

"Not really."

"Elvis. Elton. Elijah."

The boy shook his head.

"Ernie?"

"No."

"Elliot?"

"I'm not sure it works like that, Ophelia."

"But maybe you just haven't heard the correct name."

"That's true, I suppose," said the boy.

"I once had a teddy bear called Elliot," said Ophelia, which made him laugh.

She was cold. She could feel a wheeze beginning in her chest. They found a re-created Edwardian parlor. There was a comfortable settee, and a fireplace with painted fire that gave the illusion of warmth.

"We should rest awhile," said the boy.

"We should keep going," said Ophelia.

"Just for a little while."

"How did you know I would help you?"

"It was in your eyes. I knew it right away. I knew it was you who would."

"Have many children come into that room and found you there?" she asked.

"Yes," said the boy. "Over the years."

"But I still don't understand," said Ophelia, and her voice faded off. "My mum believed in everything. All sorts of stuff.

She'd know what we should do now. She died, you know, not that long ago."

"Do you miss her?" asked the boy.

"Yes," she said.

"I miss my mother too."

That made Ophelia shiver, to remember how far away from his home he was.

"Here, have this," said the boy. He removed his long embroidered coat and placed it over her shoulders.

"Won't you be cold?"

"I'll be fine."

She lifted her sleeve to check on her magical snow leopard wound. It still ached, although it was only a tiny scratch. The boy touched it gently with his fingertip.

"It will heal," he said. And he sounded very certain.

They sat for quite some time, neither of them talking. The boy raised his hand. Ophelia saw immediately the jagged scar where the missing finger should be. Her small wound was puny beside it. She looked down at her own hands in her lap.

"Did it hurt?" she whispered.

"Yes," said the boy.

"How did you do it?"

"I held it out like this for the great magical owl to eat."

"And he gave the charm in return?"

"I'll tell you," said the boy.

I held my finger out just so, and the great magical owl snapped it off like a twig. He swallowed it whole, closed his eyes, looked like he enjoyed it—the taste of it, I mean. Me? I screamed and moaned and held my bleeding hand and ripped a strip of cloth from my tunic hem and bandaged it as best I could and crouched on the ground until the first wave of pain subsided. He watched me the whole time with his cooling eyes.

The great magical owl's magic comes from his travels and his ruminations. He witnesses a sorrow, and then he thinks and thinks and thinks, and he combs his head with his claws, preens, and remembers, sometimes for days, sometimes for years. And the charm he put on me? He told me it came from his memories of the darkest of midnights, the emptiness of a palace after a plague had come, the loneliness of cemeteries, a singular wind he had once met moaning on a plain, the empty hearts of princesses who danced all night. He made this charm in the blink of an eye, placed it inside a feather. The feather drifted free from his wing, fluttered to my feet.

I know you'll wonder how a blessing might be made, but there is no equation for it, Ophelia. You will not find it in your science books. All his remaining magic, every last ounce of it that he had left in his body, he put inside a feather and then said, "Child, eat of me."

His breast heaved up and down where the arrow had pierced.

So I took the small feather, for it was really very small, and I put it on my tongue and I swallowed. I coughed. My throat was very dry. Apart from that, I didn't feel so different.

"There, it is done," said Ibrom.

"What will happen to me?" I asked.

"You will be safe now for a small while," said the owl. "Three days, three hours, and three minutes. Enough for you to make it through the forest and into the belly of the mountain."

But he was dying. Ibrom was dying, and he didn't know the charm he put on me was much more concentrated than could be imagined. I did not know it either, not for many years. The charm he bestowed upon me was grossly miscalculated.

His eyes were no longer fiery. By giving me the charm, he had broken rank. What did it matter now? He would tell me one more thing.

"The One Other has a name," he whispered.

"What did you say?" I asked.

"I know her," he hissed. "Have seen her. Have heard her name spoken."

"What is her name?" I said, and leaned closer, right beside the owl's head.

Ibrom committed one more act of treason and whispered the name to me.

Already winter was coming behind me. There was a thin gray frost spreading over the leaves. Millions upon millions of icy splinters. There was a low, chill wind. The water in the streams grew milky skins. I stood up, Ophelia, held that name close to my heart, and began to run again.

"Well?" asked Ophelia.

"Well, what?" said the boy.

He really was exasperating. He'd probably forgotten the name. It was exactly the kind of thing he'd do. If it were she who had been given the name by a dying great magical owl, she would have written it down carefully on a piece of paper and folded it three times and placed it in her pocket.

"The name?" she asked, trying not to sound angry.

The boy smiled at her slyly. "Can't you guess?"

He really was too much. She refused to guess any more names.

"Honestly," she said aloud, shaking her head. She pulled the boy's coat closer. She looked at the Edwardian parlor fire, and from the corner of her eye, she noticed again the blurriness of him. It was worse now, as though he were only half there. He seemed exhausted from just telling that story.

"You should speak your heart," said the boy, sensing.

But she didn't mention his evanescence. It seemed too hard. She had expected magic to be simple and tidy, with people disappearing in puffs of smoke—not slowly, by degrees, in a lonely, aching way.

"The thing is," she said, choosing her words carefully, "owls don't really speak, not really. I mean, only in stories, perhaps."

"The thing is," he replied, "only the right sort of people can hear them."

There was not a hint of anger in his voice. He smiled at her.

"If you do not believe in such things," he said as they got up and walked again, "then it is best I don't tell you of the troll mountain."

Ophelia didn't encourage him. She said nothing. She listened to their footsteps on the cold marble floor.

"Or how I met a giant called Gallant, who took me across

the sea on his shoulders past the meridian, the point of no return."

Ophelia stopped and looked very carefully at a display of medieval farming tools, pretending to be engrossed in a pitchfork.

"But across the sea was this kingdom, and it was here I met the King," he said.

"And the Snow Queen," said Ophelia, "who made you her prisoner."

"Yes," said the boy. "But that wasn't straightaway. Many years passed first."

"What were you doing for those years?"

"Well, mostly I played and ate sweets," said the boy.

I'd never seen mountains like the ones in the new land. Jagged, rocky mountains, not wearing a stitch of trees. Or a city as big as the one I entered that day. The town where I came from was small, and the wizard house, with its tower, was the tallest building to be seen. But here there were giant houses everywhere, with bells in their towers at each corner, and the streets teeming with people.

I searched in my satchel for the instructions. I had to search with my left hand; my right hand, with its missing finger, still ached in its bandages. I found the list of instructions but didn't read them. I'd spotted one of the last of the biscuit men that Petal had baked for me. I ate one while I thought.

After that I spent some time looking for the compass. To tell you the truth, I thought I'd lost it. I lose things easily.

My mother always said so. I was always forgetting my coat in winter and my ink pen in school, and I was always leaving my shoes on the riverbank. It seemed no amount of apologizing could appease her. I had to wait until the storm passed. Forgetting things made me feel bad. But the shoes, for instance— they were nothing important when I played in the river, which was so wide and still. The fish you could almost catch with your hands, and the blade of grass was sweet in my mouth, and every stone I skipped skipped perfectly.

Yes, it is strange that the wizards chose me.

But the compass was very important. I eventually found it in my tunic pocket, and I followed it south through the streets. Now remember, the wizards had told me in the other world I must find the just and kind ruler. And as it would happen, south took me exactly to the palace gates.

The King duly heard of my arrival. He was seated beside his nanny, who was folding his underpants very neatly. She was telling him how a walk in the garden would do him good and relieve him of his melancholy.

The King was not old as you'd expect, only a boy, much like me. He was prone to bouts of misery. There was always someone knocking on the palace door, trying to cure the King of his sadness. There was an herb man, and a man with glass jars filled with smoke, and a man with powder vials kept inside a magnificent velvet bag. And if they could not cure him, there was always someone trying a new trick. A man who juggled daggers or men dressed as women who danced in a bawdy way, or a terrible, wizened old man who charmed large green snakes.

That day he was in the throes of melancholy when the chamberlain shouted, "Your Highness!" causing the nanny to drop a whole stack of folded underpants. "There is a boy with a divine message who carries a mighty sword handed down from the angels. He says a great invasion is on the way."

The King sighed loudly. "Perhaps, Chamberlain," he said, "you would bring this boy to visit me."

When I was before the young King, he looked me up and down and sighed even louder. "They tell me you have come from a distant land, perhaps from beyond the sea," he said.

"Yes," I said, and being truthful, I still felt wobbly on my feet, because it had been a very long way. I forgot everything I was meant to say.

"And has this land got a name?" said the King, who plucked a blade of grass and began to chew it.

"Take that out of your mouth this very minute," said his nanny.

The King obeyed and put the grass down.

"Yes, it is called the Kingdom," I said. "And I come from a place called the Town."

"*This* is the Kingdom," he said, waving his arm around him. "*My* Kingdom, to be precise."

"It's a very nice kingdom," I said. "And very large and very grand."

The King looked pleased. "And your name?" he asked.

"I don't have a name," I said. "It was taken from me by the

protectorate of wizards from the east, west, and middle to keep me safe."

"No name?" said the King. "That's very unusual. Still, tell me how you came from such a faraway place. Am I to believe you walked the whole way?"

"I ran in the beginning. In the forest and the valley and through the belly of the mountain and then across the ocean."

"In a boat?" he asked, looking very bored.

"A type of boat, I suppose."

"I see," said the King. But I could tell that he didn't. "The problem is," he said, "that there is no other land across the ocean. That is only a place that exists in fairy tales. Isn't it, Nanny? Across the sea is the place you speak of when you tell me those stories at bedtime. All of which are make-believe."

The old nanny hobbled forward.

"Did you say something?" she said.

The King rolled his eyes at me. "I said, this boy here says he has come from a land across the sea and he walked the whole way here."

"Well," said the nanny, taking her glasses from her pocket and stepping closer to peer at me. "He must be very tired, and you haven't even asked him to take a seat."

He looked cross. He pointed to the grass in front of him and I sat down. "Tell me your message," said the frowning King.

"Hello," I said. "I come in friendship and mean you no harm."

The King laughed very loudly at that.

"I am a boy," I said when he had stopped laughing, "chosen

by a protectorate of wizards from the east, west, and middle to—"

"Wait," said the King. "Let me guess. You have come all this way to tell me the harvest will fail this year. You have special powers of foresight—I knew it as soon as I saw you. No, wait again, you have come all this way to tell me that a hole has opened up in the crust of the earth and we can crawl through now to the place where everyone walks on their hands."

"No," I said.

"What, then?"

"I have been chosen to deliver this sword so that the Snow Queen may be defeated." I took the very plain magical sword from its scabbard and went to hold it in the air, but as usual my arm trembled so much with the weight of it that I couldn't prize its tip from the ground.

The King was very amused.

"I have to give it to someone else, the One Other, who will help defeat the Snow Queen."

"Who is this One Other?" asked the King.

"I am not sure," I said. "The wizards said I would know the person when I found him or her. Although the great magical owl gave me a clue when he bit off my finger to put a charm on me."

Now, to the King's credit, he looked at me and tried to stop his mouth from twitching. But he lost the battle. He covered his face with his hands, and then threw his head back and roared with laughter. He grabbed his knees from the pain of it. He laughed and laughed until he wiped the tears from his eyes.

"Isn't he wonderful?" he said at last. "What shall we call him, Nanny? Shall we call him Boy?"

"Oh, he is very lovely," said the old nanny. "Should I make up a nice, soft bed for Boy, seeing he has come such a long way?"

"Yes," he said. "Yes, Nanny, I think that would be a good idea indeed."

I cannot complain about the care I was given. The royal tailor was called that very first day and was told I should be attired in only the finest things: brocade velvets and coats embroidered with golden birds and the best silk stockings. The nanny combed my hair in the way that was the style. A man was employed to do nothing but wash my face with a warm flannel whenever it was required. I ate every type of food that could be imagined. The small room beside the King's was made up with a new bed with satin cushions and covers.

"Whatever you want, you shall have," said the young King, "as long as you stay and be my friend."

"What of my message?" I asked.

"Oh, we will talk more of it later," he said. "For now I command you to be my friend."

Each time I spoke of leaving, the King grew petulant.

"I command you to stay," he said. "I command you to play that game again. The one where you pretend to be a boy from another land. It's ever so funny. Everything was so tiresome before you came."

I thought of my home. I won't lie. Each night, I took the

magical sword the wizards had entrusted me with and held it heavy in my hands. I wondered for hours of what I should do. I wrote great stories in my head in which I escaped and found the One Other. But I never left the bed. Each time we went through the streets or to parties or to dances on the royal litter, I looked at the crowd. I looked at each and every person. I tried to imagine them with the sword. I looked for something in their eyes that made them capable of defeating the Snow Queen, although I had no idea what that might be.

Each day I was entertained by jugglers and fire-eaters and poets and storytellers. Yet each night I thought of my mother, and my heart ached. Each night I tried to remember my name.

"Do not despair," said the nanny when she tucked me into bed each night. "One day you will return home again."

"But for now I command him to stay here," said the King from the next room. "Because otherwise who would I have to talk to at night?"

Each night the King spoke through the little wall that separated our bedrooms. He spoke, sometimes for hours, of his worries. He worried about the world. People kept wanting to go off exploring it, and sometimes these people never came back. He was worried about his headaches, and maybe he was about to start having visions because he heard this was what happened.

"The wizards had visions," I said.

"What of?" asked the King.

"Of my journey. It was a bit murky in parts. The Great Wizard said it was like looking into a brown river."

"Did these wizards teach you anything magical?" asked the young King.

"Not really," I said. "I mean, only how to listen to the Herald Trees, I suppose."

"A Herald Tree," he said after a very long pause, because he must have been growing sleepy. He yawned. "I think I own one of those."

The Herald Tree was in the farthest reach of the King's garden, and we rode there the very next day on our elephants. Oh yes, the King had imported elephants. He was always doing things like that.

"I haven't been here for a very long time," said the King. "But my father showed it to me once. He said it was a very rare tree. It had been given to my mother and father on their wedding day. It was from a distant place. I am sure it was called . . . what did you call it?"

"A Herald Tree," I said, not wanting him to be wrong.

The King opened up a rusty door hidden by vine, and we entered a tiny walled garden. In the middle of the walled garden was the tree. It was a smallish tree, stout, with a bulbous trunk and spreading crown of glossy, dark leaves.

The first time I placed my hand on it, I heard everything. The King spoke endlessly. The birds sang mercilessly. There was the distant rumbling of the royal thoroughfare. I separated all these things out and found the emptiness, just the way the wizards had taught me. In the emptiness I heard Petal first. Petal, clear as day, laughing.

"You must not forget us," she said.

The King interrupted by tapping me on the shoulder.

"What do you do that for?" he asked. The truth was he didn't like anything that didn't involve him.

"It's the way the wizards speak across distances," I said.

That made the King laugh heartily. He sat down on the grass and rested his back against the wall. "I command you, listen again," he said. "And see what they have to tell us."

I placed my hand on the tree once more. "Do not forget steadfastness, child. Remember the sword. Remember your cause," said the Great Wizard, almost as though he were whispering in my ear. Then more voices:

"One of your ponytails is higher than the other."

"That always happens when I have to do it myself."

"You'll get better at it."

I listened to these voices and was very confused.

Then suddenly there came the slicing, scraping sound of a sleigh, the trampling of hooves, great wings, monstrous wings, the screeches of owls. I leapt back from the tree and held my hand as though it had been burnt.

"What?" asked the King.

"I heard the Snow Queen," I said. After all, the wizards had taught me to always tell the truth. "She is close."

The King slapped his thigh and doubled over. "You never stop, do you?" he laughed. "Now we must ride back to the castle because I feel like playing another game."

It was hide-and-seek; then we rode boats on the river stocked specially with rainbow-colored fish. This was followed by quoits and checkers and badminton. Each and every day, as soon as one game was finished, the King thought of another.

I was treated by the King's visiting physicians whenever I looked a little sad. It felt to me as though a tide had gone out: the memories that had always shimmered just beneath the surface receded. I thought of my mother, you see, and the thought didn't hurt me. I didn't cry. I didn't ache. The days passed. The weeks passed. The months passed. Years.

11

In which Ophelia and the boy
are chased by wolves

———◆———

Ophelia and the boy were standing in the arcade of mirrors. There were mirrors as large as houses and mirrors shaped like stars that divided them again and again until they were almost nothing. There were mirrors that made them tall as giants and others that made them short and stout. The boy looked at himself in a long mirror. He held out his arms.

"What's happening to me?" he whispered.

He'd noticed it, and the fact made Ophelia's heart sink. He was looking at his reflection, at the blurring of his edges, as though the outside of him were smudged.

"I'm not sure," said Ophelia. "Maybe it's the charm wearing off?"

She tried to think of something comforting to say to a disappearing boy, but it was difficult. It was while she was thinking that she heard a long, mournful howl. The boy froze where he stood before the mirror, arms raised, examining himself.

"What was that?" whispered Ophelia.

Another long howl, a frenzy of baying in return. It was close, very close. The boy unfroze, turned to Ophelia, his eyes filled with terror.

"Wolves," he whispered. "They know I am free. We must run."

They ran. They ran through *Seventeenth-Century Ceramics*, where the teacups rattled on the shelves, through a room filled with marble bodies, arms outstretched, through *A Millennium of Religious Hats*, the mitres trembling slightly with their passing footsteps. Through the largest collection of thimbles in the world, past triptychs, past trombones. Past mummified cats, past miniature paintings, past *Yurts and Yaks: Life in Mongolia.*

"Why are there wolves?" cried Ophelia as they ran. "Where have they come from?"

"They are the Queen's wolves," said the boy.

They ran through *Mysteries of the Aztecs, The Hunter Through Time,* and Ophelia accidentally knocked over a pile of spears stacked haphazardly against a wall.

"I don't understand," she cried.

"Stop trying to," said the boy.

The howling was now very close.

Too close.

The boy changed tack suddenly, leaping onto a long, dark staircase and shutting the door after Ophelia. They ran to the first landing and crouched in the shadows.

"What should we do?" whispered Ophelia.

"I don't know," said the boy, which didn't offer her much faith.

They heard footsteps then—not human footsteps but the drumming feet of running dogs, which was a noise Ophelia had never heard before. A scratching, pounding, smacking sound.

"What's that?" she said. She hoped he wasn't going to say wolves. But she didn't have to wait for his reply. The door to the stairwell burst open, and on the landing above, she saw the crouched shapes of them.

"Quickly!" shouted the boy, pulling her by the arm.

They were at least three times her size. She saw that before she turned, pulled by the boy. There were several of them, a hulking, skulking, moving mass. Green eyes glowing. Wolves. Most definitely, impossibly wolves. Wild wolves roaming in a museum. Now, what would Max Lowenstein say about that?

Don't look back, said her mother urgently in her ear. *Just run.*

Ophelia and the boy entered an exhibition of crowns, and they slammed the door shut behind them. They heard the thud of the wolves against the wood, the scratching of their nails.

"We need to get away from them," panted Ophelia. "We need to get to another floor quickly."

"Yes," he panted back. "They'll be through in no time."

Behind the exhibition of crowns there was a small cafeteria. They raced around the tables and chairs, knocking over a stand of chips, then tumbled into the kitchen. They heard the gallery door slam open and the wolves leaping into the room.

"Oh dear," squeaked Ophelia.

Her eyes scanned the room. There was no elevator, there was no exit. The cafeteria was a dead end.

"Backward," she screeched. "Garbage chute."

The wolves were in the cafeteria now. They moved toward them slowly, growling low. The largest of them, with wild green eyes, came forward sleekly, its gray fur erect. It snarled, showing its fangs.

"I'm scared of wolves," whispered Ophelia.

The boy was lifting up the garbage chute door.

"Quickly," he said.

Ophelia dived in headfirst and began to slide away into the darkness. She heard the boy shouting.

"A charm was bestowed upon me by Ibrom, the great magical owl, who I shot through the heart with my arrow!" he shouted. "You cannot harm me until the final hour."

She knew he would be holding up his hand, his missing finger exposed.

But he didn't sound so sure. She could hear the wolves howling.

"Hurry!" she yelled as she slid away in the blackness, twisting and turning between the floors. She put out her hands and managed to stop herself from falling farther by turning sideways and stretching across the tunnel.

She heard the clang of the chute's metal door. Had he made it?

"Oh, please, please, please," she whispered. She heard the soft, rushing noise of something sliding toward her. "Oh, please, please, please."

A hard thud. She was knocked from her position by the boy. They slid together through the darkness, not speaking.

Finally, "Are you okay?"

"Yes," he replied. "But it really stinks in here."

Ophelia and the boy used the exit in the large museum refectory. They dropped to the ground soundlessly and looked into each other's eyes.

"What will we do?" whispered the boy.

"The ghosts said the wolves were afraid of them, that they'd never go to the sixth floor," Ophelia whispered in reply.

Good thinking, whispered her mother, which made Ophelia, despite everything, smile.

They could no longer hear the wolves but didn't want to chance taking the elevators.

The stairwells were as confusing as every other part of the museum. The first murky set took them only as far as the third floor, where they had to creep through several dark galleries. The next staircase, with green marble and gold banisters, took them as far as the fifth.

Ophelia sighed loudly, extracted her map. They crouched together over it until they found the closest staircase, which inexplicably began behind a plain wooden door in an exhibition of sewing baskets.

At last the polar bear reared up before them, and even though she knew it wasn't alive, Ophelia found herself reaching out to clutch the boy's arm. He felt real. He did. The boy was flesh and bones, yet if she looked at him from the corner of her eye, he was so faded that she could almost see the teetering stack of sewing machines through him.

They squeezed themselves through racks of ball gowns, picked their way over a pile of birdcages, around several chests overflowing with gold coins, past more merry-go-round horses with melancholy eyes.

They heard the very distant baying of wolves.

"We're nearly there," said Ophelia. "We just need to find the door. It's in here somewhere. Then the wolves won't follow us."

The boy agreed. He was paler now. He looked exhausted. He walked slowly behind Ophelia. They moved between several rows of farm equipment (now, where had *that* come from?), clambered over a pile of life buoys (they weren't here last time), stepped gingerly through an expanse of colored glass bottles (definitely not here before!). Try as they might, they could not find the door.

"Everything's different," she said. "Almost everything. I don't know how it could be, but it is. The polar bear was there and the sewing machines and the ball gowns. But there's all this new stuff, and everything has changed position. There were these flags last time, and all these paintings, and a big anchor as tall as the roof, and I can't even see that this time. And the door was right at the end, but now I can't even see the end."

"It's her sorcery," said the boy.

"Will they find us?" asked Ophelia.

"I'm not sure."

"I don't want to be eaten by a wolf."

"No," said the boy, with all the comfort he could muster.

"My mother loved stories about wolves. She wrote them all the time."

"Yes."

"It's just—didn't the wizards teach you anything about what to do in a situation like this? I mean, something magical."

They had stopped in front of a very fancy carriage. The boy opened the carriage door and they climbed up inside. They sat side by side. The carriage was near a window, and they looked out at the city still in darkness, with a tiny sliver of gray light on the horizon. Oh, how frozen it was.

"Only what I've told you," said the boy. "About telling the truth, and being still and feeling the earth through your feet, and helping anyone that needs help. And how to hear the Snow Queen, of course, or smell her or sense her from a long way off. And how to listen to the Herald Trees. And to never give up, even when you seem lonely and a long way from home."

"Not how to make yourself invisible or anything?"

"No," said the boy.

Ophelia slumped back into the seat and covered her eyes.

"You mustn't give up," said the boy. "All will be saved if we find the sword."

He looked deathly pale. He rested his head against the carriage glass and shivered. Ophelia took the coat and laid it across him.

"I need to find my father," she said. "I have to get there before he realizes I'm gone. I need to tell him everything. He'll know what to do about the wolves. He has to listen to me. He'll help me search. I'll come back as soon as I can."

She touched the boy's sleeve, because it shimmered in the first morning light, as though it were not a real thing but a ghost of a thing.

The boy took her hands. It didn't feel odd. Not the way it would have felt odd if any other boy held both her hands. Like, say, Max Lowenstein from the Children's Science Society of Greater London, where she went on Tuesday nights. Max was nice to talk to and knew a lot about the taxonomy of cats, but she never, ever would have let him hold her hands.

She could feel the space where the boy's finger was missing, eaten by the great magical owl.

"Ophelia," said the boy. "Don't go, not yet. I have more to tell you."

One day the King came to me, Ophelia, wearing a very serious expression. There had been rumors for some time, whispered in the royal corridors, spoken of over pots boiling in the kitchen, mentioned in hushed voices by chambermaids, and the King could no longer ignore them.

"Boy," he said. "I have something I must say to you."

I was frightened by his serious gaze.

"I have noticed," said the King. "And others also . . ."

"What?" I asked.

"It's a strange thing," he said. "And in the beginning I didn't believe it to be true."

Again he stopped.

"*What?*" I asked again.

"What I mean to say," said the King, "and I don't mean to

cause you any alarm . . . what I mean to say is you, my faithful friend, have been here nearly six years and you haven't grown at all."

I looked down at myself.

"You have not changed. You have not aged. You're exactly the same as the day you arrived. The royal barber says even your hair has not grown. Don't you think this is strange?"

It was true. I couldn't argue. I hadn't grown up at all. The King, who had turned seventeen, had grown taller and thinner. He had sprouted a fine, downy mustache. But me, I hadn't changed at all. I was exactly the same size and height as when I arrived. My hair was the same length, my eyes the same color and clarity, my skin the skin of an eleven-year-old boy.

"But I told you already," I said, and I'd told him it many times. "It was the charm put on me by the great magical owl. It was meant to keep me safe for three days and three hours and three minutes, but I think, perhaps, it was spun wrong and now has lasted longer."

The King tilted his head to one side and smiled. He did that whenever I spoke of my journey. He called the two highest priests in the kingdom. They poked and prodded me, and asked me great and convoluted questions about God and the angels that I couldn't answer.

"It is certainly unusual," said the second highest of the priests. "Would you say miraculous, Your Holiness?"

The highest of the priests didn't like to waste the word *miraculous* on trifling matters. He would much rather save it for large balls of fire ripping through the sky or people resurrected from graves, all of which hardly ever happened. And also it was a Thursday, and nothing miraculous ever happened on Thursdays.

"Marvelous, perhaps," the highest priest said. "But not miraculous. He will need to be monitored."

Right then I remembered again my reason for being there, as was sometimes the case, and the words rushed out, exactly the way the wizards had taught me.

"I come in friendship and mean you no harm. I am a boy chosen by a protectorate of wizards from the east, west, and middle to deliver this sword"—I went to hold up the sword. Where was it? It was under the bed, collecting dust—"so that the Snow Queen may be defeated."

It was a very hot day. The King laughed and waved his golden fan before his face. "Ah yes, the Snow Queen," he said. "This snow we are waiting for."

I must have looked despondent.

"Now, now," said the King. "To cheer you up, I will declare today the Festival of the Marvelous Boy."

"Oh, please, no," I said.

"There will be a procession in the street, and you will be carried in a great chair. Chancellor, quickly see that a chair is built of gold. Each year, on this day, you will be paraded. And each year we will see if you have changed. There will be music and dancing and food."

"I don't want to," I said.

"I command it," said the King.

So each year from that day, the Festival of the Marvelous Boy was held. I was made to dress in my splendid coat and carry my sword—which the King offered to dip in silver, but which I declined.

Each year it was true: I did not age. Each year I was paraded through the streets, and the crowd cheered and danced and sang. The land was more prosperous than it had ever been: the King's coffers were filled with gold, and the crops grew tall, and there was no one hungry. Everyone put it down to me, the strange, ageless friend of the King.

Each year I stood beside the King, who shouted, "People, our friend from the other Land, all hail the Marvelous Boy."

The crowd cheered so loudly that I could not hear, but all I felt was empty and unfathomably sad.

"But when does the Snow Queen arrive?" asked Ophelia. She was still holding the boy's hand. His skin was pale as snow. His eyes closed as he spoke.

She came when the King was twenty. An emissary from a distant land came to offer the hand of the ruling monarch's eldest daughter. She was, by all accounts, the most beautiful girl in the entire world. The King scratched his head and said, "Not another one."

"You should consider it, sir," said the chancellor. "It is said that this land is famous for its diamonds and other glittering gems, and for its perfect furs."

"At least a meeting," said the royal ambassador to all other realms.

"What do you think, Nanny?" asked the King.

"Well, I suppose it wouldn't do any harm," she replied.

"What do you think, Boy?"

"She is probably very nice," I replied.

She came in a white coach with a silvery trim, pulled by seven white horses. She wore a glittering white gown and a sparkling crown in her white-blond hair. She carried a large and glittering sword in a jewel-encrusted scabbard. When the King saw her, he fell in love immediately. He felt at once as though he were falling and flying. He couldn't breathe. The princess disembarked from her coach and held out her delicate, pale hand.

"You are enchanted to meet me," the princess said.

The King was.

He could not eat, he could not sleep. He could not sit down, he could not stand. He moaned and rolled on his bed. He held his head in his hands. Oh, how he was violently sick with love.

He forgot about me.

Now, when I first saw the princess, I too almost fell to my knees. It was not because of her great beauty, although very beautiful she was. She was coming down the long golden walk, you see, flanked by her courtiers and her maids-in-waiting and her collection of miniature white poodles, which snapped and snarled at everyone who passed.

She stopped.

I stopped.

She smiled.

Her best, least wicked smile.

And I knew immediately who she was.

"I know of this charm," she said to me when we were alone. It was after the first time I had tried to escape. "Which my not-so-faithful servant Ibrom bestowed upon you. Not three days, as you have told the King, but three hundred and three years."

"Three hundred and three years?" I whispered, the air knocked out of me by her words.

"Yes, you will live that long, and I will not be able to harm you until the charm is gone. When it is, I can run you through with my sword, the Great Sorrow. You have heard of her, haven't you? The wizards will have told you all about her, no? They will have seen my sword in their pathetic little visions."

A prison room was built for me. The King asked that the picture of my marvelous life be painted on the wall, with my name in very big letters, arched just so.

"Can we still have the Festival of the Marvelous Boy?" he asked.

"I will consider it," said the Queen.

My sword was taken from me to be destroyed. I tried to look at the King, to catch his eye, but he wouldn't look at me. Then the Queen closed the door and locked it with her golden key.

Each year at the Festival of the Marvelous Boy, a crowd came. I was allowed from my room to stand on the little stage. Each year I looked at the faces. I looked into the eyes of the children, each and every one of them, but I recognized none of them. None of them seemed right.

Each year the crowd grew smaller.

Fewer faces to look at and hope for.

The King grew old. When he visited, he walked with a cane. He kept a key to my room. Each time he came, it was as though he had something to say. But when he arrived, it was as though he had forgotten it. He came and sat beside my bed and said nothing.

"Will you not let me go?" I asked.

The King said, "You know, Boy, you know very well I could not disobey her."

The snow did not end. It fell and fell and fell until the land was white, and the children grew hungry.

"Do you see now what has happened?"

The King lowered his ancient shoulders and began to cry. "Yes, I see it now."

"Did you really destroy the sword?" I asked gently now, for I hated to see him so sad.

"No, Boy. I did not destroy it. I pretended I was taking it to be destroyed but then hid it quickly when she wasn't looking. I hid it first in the elephant stables. They all froze, you know. Then later, years later, I hid it in the gardens. Then much, much later, in a junk room. After that . . . well, it was a very long time ago and I don't at all remember where. I have looked for it myself now and been unable to find it."

"Don't worry, then," I said. "As long as it still exists, all will be well in the end."

＊　＊　＊

"The sun is nearly up," said Ophelia.

The boy opened his eyes.

"I know you will find the sword, Ophelia," he said, with great certainty. "I know you will find the sword and the Snow Queen will be defeated."

12

*In which Ophelia meets
Miss Kaminski again*

———◆———

Ophelia left the boy in the carriage and ran down the staircases between the floors. The dawn light was filling up the galleries. The painted angels were swimming to life. Straightaway Ophelia noticed something was afoot in the museum. Everywhere the old guards were on the move. They were marching in and out of rooms, with their large black handbags by their sides. They had scowls on their faces. They were kneeling down and looking into the heating vents, peering into the huge urns, lifting up and looking behind curtains. Ophelia leapt into a public elevator just in time.

She raced along the corridors, sped downstairs, upstairs, in and out of rooms. And before she could stop her feet, she had raced straight into the pavilion of wolves.

She skidded to a halt on the marble floor. She stayed very still, barely breathing. The wolves looked back at her with their dull glass eyes. They didn't move. They were their usual mangy, threadbare selves.

"Okay," Ophelia said to herself. "Everything is fine."

She took a squirt on her puffer, then took one step backward slowly. The wolves did not move. Another squirt, another step.

She ran through the small circular library and out the other side. She raced down the long, thin gallery of painted girls in party dresses. She trembled with the cold. They really should do something about the heating in this stupid museum, she thought, and then froze.

"Miss Kaminski," cried Ophelia. "You gave me such a fright."

"Forgive me, Ophelia," said the curator. She said her name very precisely, in a way that made Ophelia shiver even more.

Miss Kaminski smiled, but Ophelia thought she didn't really look sorry to have given such a scare. She looked secretly pleased.

She knelt down. Her buttermilk-colored suit made a sighing sound. She smiled her beautiful smile again. She held Ophelia just below the shoulders. She had icy hands. Ophelia could feel them even through her blue velvet jacket.

"You're very early in your wanderings today," said Miss Kaminski. "And look, without any shoes."

Ophelia looked down at her stocking feet. "I stayed with Daddy last night, here in the museum," she said. "And I just thought I'd run very quickly to see the . . . dinosaurs."

"Oh yes, the dinosaurs," said Miss Kaminski.

Up close like that, Ophelia noticed there were tiny spidery lines around Miss Kaminski's eyes. She looked young and old at the same time. Her eyes were the palest blue. Her frosty pink lipstick was a little smudged at the corners. Miss Kaminski searched Ophelia's face as though she was looking for something.

She had a fresh, clean smell like washed and sun-dried sheets, and something else, something sweeter. It tickled Ophelia's nose.

"Did you like the dinosaurs again?" she said. "You have not grown tired of them yet?"

"Oh no. I'd never grow tired of them."

"What else have you been doing so early in the morning?" the curator asked. Her hands squeezed Ophelia's shoulders. She squeezed while she smiled very sweetly.

"Oh, nothing, really," whispered Ophelia.

Miss Kaminski's long, pale fingers, with her immaculate, polished nails, were hurting her.

"Ouch," said Ophelia.

Suddenly she felt very small. She felt very small in that vast museum. All the painted girls with their lonely, bored faces looked down at her. They looked at her as though they had seen it all before. Ophelia's breath puffed in front of her, but the museum curator's breath did not. Ophelia saw it hover in front of her mouth, a small, polite mist.

"Do you miss your mummy?" whispered Miss Kaminski.

The pain was very bad in Ophelia's shoulders now.

Tears welled up in her eyes. She couldn't stop them. She looked at the white floor. She looked at the painted girls. She looked at the ceiling.

Miss Kaminski leaned forward. She placed her lips on

Ophelia's forehead and kissed her there. She didn't remove them. Ophelia felt a tightness in her chest. Every breath that she had was being pressed gradually out of her.

"I hope," said Miss Kaminski slowly, as she squeezed the breath out of Ophelia, "you are being a very good little girl."

After this, she stood up.

"I think now you should go back to your father's workroom, and you should sit on a chair and stay out of harm's way."

Ophelia couldn't answer. Her chest was too tight. She felt as though she had been drenched through with cold rain and left to dry in a winter wind. She quivered and coughed a tiny, little cough.

Miss Kaminski took her by the hand. She led her down the stairs and through the *Gallery of Time.* She pulled Ophelia down the damp and creaking stairs to her father's workroom.

Each step. One foot after the other.

Down.

Down.

Down.

Ophelia became aware of something. The sweet, warm scent that Miss Kaminski wore was exactly the scent of hot chocolate.

The curator pulled her roughly by the arm.

"Hurry up," she said.

In the sword workroom, Mr. Whittard jumped up. A sheaf of papers cascaded onto the floor. He straightened his eyebrows, ran a hand through his hair, stood at attention, his mouth hanging open at the sight of Miss Kaminski.

"M-m-miss Kaminski," he stammered.

"Mr. Whittard," said Miss Kaminski.

Ophelia stood between them, trembling. She retrieved her inhaler and took a puff.

Mr. Whittard looked at Ophelia and looked at the old throne, where the blankets still lay with the shoes sticking out at the end.

"Your daughter," said Miss Kaminski in an icy voice, and she delivered Ophelia the way one would a parcel. "A reminder, Mr. Whittard, my sword will arrive today, and I trust that all your preparations are in order."

She turned on her stiletto heel and left.

"Ophelia Jane," he said. "Where have you been?"

"I went to the bathroom," she said, and then convulsed with shivers.

"Are you telling the truth?" he said, wrapping her in his arms.

She remembered what the boy had told her. *Always tell the truth.* "No," she said.

"Where have you been?" Mr. Whittard asked. "I thought you were lying right there on that chair. I can't believe it. I thought you were there. I've been so busy, but I thought you were lying there."

"We're in great danger," Ophelia said. "Great, great, great danger."

"Goodness me, what kind of danger?" asked Mr. Whittard.

"In danger of the Snow Queen's army waking up and freezing the whole world and making everything sad. I've met a boy who is a prisoner, and he has lived for a long time, and he was sent all the way here to give the sword to someone else, but they took the sword ages ago. And all they feed him is porridge. They were keeping him locked in a room, but I've let him out. I was chased by snow leopards and helped by a ghost and nearly eaten by a misery bird. Just now we were chased by wolves. Did you hear them howling? I have to find the sword, and I have to find the One Other who can wield it before the stroke of six."

Mr. Whittard stared at his daughter for a while. He hugged her close to his chest, then looked at her again.

Ophelia stared back at him. Her eyes filled with tears.

"Oh, darling. You do take after your mother."

"We're in great danger," whispered Ophelia. "Didn't you hear the wolves?"

"You've got a fever," said Mr. Whittard. He felt his daughter's forehead, which was burning. "I'm taking you back to the hotel."

He scooped her up in his arms and carried her through the vast and monumental corridors, down the grand staircases. He carried her across the glittering wedding mosaic floor in the foyer. That morning Ophelia fancied she could hear the Wintertide Clock ticking. It seemed to be shaking the whole building. She tried to speak, feebly, to tell her father more, but he was already carrying her through the great revolving doors, out into the snow.

At that very moment the museum guards were fanning out from the elevator on the sixth floor. The Snow Queen waited quietly while they searched in every corner. Beside her was Mr. Pushkinova, his head bowed. When they at last opened the carriage door, the Snow Queen strode forward.

"Did you really think that scrap of a girl could help you?" she said to the boy. "A little girl who squeaks like a mouse?"

Then she began to laugh, her terrible, clear, tinkling-bell laugh.

· PART THREE ·

13

In which Ophelia is very ill and Alice is very upset, but they come to a mutual agreement

———◆———

I feel better," said Ophelia, lying in her hotel bed. "I swear, I feel better."

"Your temperature is through the roof," said Mr. Whittard. "You'll have to stay here. All morning. Don't even start to argue. Alice, you'll stay here too."

"I can't!" screeched Alice. "I'm having my hair done and my dress fitting, and then my portrait is being hung. Miss Kaminski is going to teach me how to hold the special shears and cut the ribbon."

"You'll be staying here," said Mr. Whittard. "And speaking of special things, Miss Kaminski's prized sword is arriving today and I am meant to be there right now, making preparations."

"Don't you understand?" wailed Alice. "I need to be beautiful."

"You're nearly sixteen," said her father, very calmly. "You

need to start acting like an adult. You're to stay here and keep an eye on your little sister."

Alice slumped down in front of the mirror. She stared at Ophelia lying on the bed. "You always ruin everything," she said.

Ophelia wanted to say something, but she couldn't. She felt weak and small. She coughed. She felt as though she were falling, falling backward a long way, and there was nothing she could do to stop it. She watched the snow drifting past the window.

She didn't know how long she slept.

In her dream her mother was calling her.

Her mother's voice was coming from deep within the museum, and Ophelia was running, trying to find her. Sometimes the voice seemed closer and she would think, I don't have far to go. Then the voice would fade. Finally, when she was near the *Gallery of Time*, she heard her mother say her name so clearly that she stopped still.

Susan Worthington was sitting on a chair near one of the windows just outside the gallery. She was sitting the way she always sat, with her legs crossed and a book in her lap. She didn't look sick. She didn't look sick at all, and that filled Ophelia with happiness. Her mother's long brown hair was undone and blow-dried, just the way she wore it when she went to the movies or to dinner. She had lipstick on. Her mother never wore lipstick unless something very special was about to happen.

"Mum," Ophelia cried. "Mummy!"

She rushed toward her mother and was embraced. She smelt her. Her cinnamony, rosy, clean-haired, ink-stained smell. Her mother smoothed back Ophelia's hair and gazed at her face. She took Ophelia's glasses and wiped the tears from her eyes. She cleaned the smudges from Ophelia's glasses with the hem of her skirt.

"Now, you have a busy few hours ahead of you," said her mother, "if you are going to save this world."

"Do you believe it all?" asked Ophelia.

"Of course I believe it all," said her mother.

"But I don't know what to do."

"You do," said Susan Worthington.

"Should I think scientifically?"

"You should think with your heart," said her mother.

"My heart?" whispered Ophelia.

"Your heart," said her mother, and she touched Ophelia's chest with the tip of her finger. It was the tiniest of touches, but a warmth and new hope spread through Ophelia's body. She began to smile.

Then her mother looked behind her. There was another voice calling Ophelia, a very loud, very angry voice.

Ophelia spun around and woke up with a start. Alice was sitting in a chair by the window, yelling.

"Why wouldn't you wake up?" Alice said. "You were shouting so much. Shouting out, *Mum, mum, mum.* And you were crying and then laughing."

"Sorry," said Ophelia.

She looked at her watch. She had been asleep for hours. It

was nearly midday. Would the special sword have arrived at the museum? Her mother had been gone three months, nine days, and eleven hours.

"I feel much better," said Ophelia. She looked at her arm for the magical snow leopard scratch and it was completely gone.

"Good for you," said Alice, taking her place in front of the mirror again.

"Have you heard of mutualism?"

"Shut up," said Alice. "You're annoying me."

The old Alice would have never said, "Shut up." The old Alice would have said, "You can tell me about mutualism if you let me braid your hair."

"Well, it's a type of symbiosis," said Ophelia. "Where two animals live together and help each other in a way that is mutually beneficial."

"I'm ignoring you."

"Like the red-billed oxpecker eating the ticks off an impala."

No response. Alice applied her lipstick now.

"What I'm saying is, why *should* you have to miss out on everything?" said Ophelia.

Alice raised her delicately arched eyebrows.

She was paler now, paler than Ophelia could ever remember her being. So pale that fragile blue veins showed beside her eyes. Ophelia looked at her sister's reflection in the mirror and saw she was very beautiful. Not the pretty, rosy kind of beauty that she had arrived with. This new beauty was much brighter and much cooler.

"I'll come back to the museum with you," said Ophelia, "and

you'll get to have your hair and everything done, and I prom-ise I won't tell Dad if you don't tell him that I am there."

Alice watched her with sparkling blue eyes.

"I have a lot of things that I have to do, important things," said Ophelia. "Just like you. All I'm saying is, why should we *both* miss out?"

"I'll be toast if Dad finds out," said Alice.

"He'll never know," said Ophelia.

Alice started to hum her tuneless song and continued painting her lips. Ophelia climbed out of bed. The word *toast* had made her hungry. Her stomach grumbled. She made toast and sat at the little breakfast table. She opened a new tin of sardines and carefully placed some on her toast. She knew she would need every ounce of strength. She wondered what Lucy Coutts ate the day she rescued the baby in the runaway stroller and became a hero.

After her toast she found the hotel sewing kit in the bath-room, and even though she wasn't sure how to stitch properly, she turned her blue velvet coat inside out and sewed up the hole in her right-hand pocket. She had a feeling she would need a pocket. It was jagged stitching, but it made her feel good.

Alice came to the door, and Ophelia waited for what she would say.

"Let's go," her sister said.

14

*In which the Great Sorrow is delivered to
the museum, and Ophelia does not realize that Alice
is about to be placed in the Snow Queen's machine*

———◆———

Alice and Ophelia trudged toward the museum. Alice wore a white fur coat and white jeans and silver heels that were way too grown-up for her. Ophelia was in the clothes she had worn all night and all the day before. Her braids were coming undone, and her glasses were very smudgy. The snow was falling so hard and fast that they could barely see. Ophelia wheezed in the frozen air.

On the wedding mosaic floor they parted ways.

"Promise me you won't tell," said Ophelia.

"I promise," said Alice, but she was already staring past her sister as though she were hardly there at all.

Ophelia went to the sword exhibition hall and crept carefully along the corridor. She wanted to see this arriving sword firsthand. It might just be the boy's sword. She felt cross, not having thought of that before. She could hear her father's voice as she entered the room and pressed herself behind one of the heavy velvet drapes that covered each window.

There was her father, waiting as a large wooden crate was wheeled into the gallery. He was breathing into his gloved hands, stamping his cold feet inside his boots in the huge, freezing room. Miss Kaminski, who did not seem to feel the cold, watched as the crate was brought to the center of the room to the raised platform.

"Now, shall I show you our prize?" said Miss Kaminski.

The crate was broken open, and the great and glorious sword was revealed.

"She is beautiful, is she not, Mr. Whittard?" said Miss Kaminski. Ophelia saw that at first her father couldn't speak. The sword shimmered with the brilliance of a million diamonds. It sparkled and glinted, and the light danced and spun around it.

"Why have I never heard of this sword?" her father whispered at last. "I have studied the great swords of the world since I was a boy, and not once has such a magnificent sword been mentioned."

"It has been our little secret." Miss Kaminski smiled, walking around the glass case, the light of the sword playing on her skin. "And tonight the world will learn of her at last."

What would the world learn? Ophelia stayed hidden behind the curtain as Miss Kaminski passed, high heels clicking across the marble floor, shouting instructions to the men as she went.

What do you think? Ophelia's mother said quietly.

"I think she's very, very bad," whispered Ophelia in return.

You must find the boy and find the sword and find the One Other, said her mother. *You don't have much time.*

"I know," said Ophelia. "I know."

She slid out from behind the curtain and sped across the gallery to the exit. She was prepared for getting lost on the way. Even with a map the museum was impossible.

As she raced along the corridors, she saw that the guards had gone back to knitting and dozing. But the museum had also started to fill with people, more people than Ophelia had ever seen before. Tour groups were being led up and down the staircases. A long line was growing outside the *Gallery of Time.* She squeezed herself through and saw that the little window at the base of the clock still contained the number 1.

She wasn't too late. She still had time.

She took a squirt on her puffer and climbed a small staircase two steps at a time to where she thought the elevator to the sixth floor normally stood, but instead found a gallery of dresses. It was a very large gallery, with chandeliers blazing, and ball gowns and wedding dresses and tea gowns hanging everywhere behind glass.

Ophelia was about to turn to race back down the steps when she heard Alice's voice, followed by Miss Kaminski's laughter.

"Really, Alice," said Miss Kaminski. "You are delightful."

Ophelia moved forward quietly into the gallery.

Alice was sitting before a mirror, and a hairdresser was fixing her hair into loops and curls, strung with shining beads, as Miss Kaminski watched. Alice wore a white gown covered in crystals, which glittered and gleamed in the chandelier light.

"It's so beautiful," she said. "And it fits me perfectly."

"I am very pleased," Miss Kaminski said.

Ophelia saw a man enter the room from a far door. It was Mr. Pushkinova—she knew straightaway. His milky eyes made her shudder. In his hands he carried a cushion, and on the cushion was a delicate tiara.

Ophelia didn't like the way he bowed and sneered at her sister.

"One of the prettiest yet, ma'am," he said, and bowed again.

"She is beyond pretty," said Miss Kaminski. "Has her painting been hung yet, Mr. Pushkinova?"

"I have just hung it this very moment," said Mr. Pushkinova.

"Very good."

"Can I look at it yet?" asked Alice.

"Soon," said Miss Kaminski.

The museum curator nodded at Mr. Pushkinova and the hairdresser to leave the room. Ophelia's feet stayed rooted to the ground. She should leave. Her head told her to leave. Time was counting down. The hands on the Wintertide Clock were tick, tick, ticking. She should leave, but she just couldn't make her feet move.

"Would you like to have everything, Alice?" asked Miss Kaminski. "Everything that you ever wanted?"

"Like clothes and stuff?" asked Alice.

"Anything and everything."

"Yes," said Alice. "I mean, who wouldn't?"

It was like being in a dream, thought Ophelia, this inability to move. She knew something bad was going to happen. She was going to hear Alice say something terrible.

Miss Kaminski said, "Can you forget your family, Alice?"

Alice opened her mouth to speak, then stopped.

Ophelia watched her stare into her reflection. Alice was meant to look after her. Susan Worthington had spoken to Alice before she died.

"You must always look after Ophelia," she had said. "You don't have to be her mother, but you have to look out for her. This is, above everything else, what I need you to do."

Alice hadn't wanted to listen. She had put her hands over her ears and shouted: *"You are not going to die."*

Ophelia watched Miss Kaminski watching Alice thinking. Time slowed down. Ophelia forgot to breathe.

"Yes," said Alice. "I can forget them all."

To which Miss Kaminski laughed.

"Wonderful," she said. "You must come with me, then. There is something I would very much like to show you."

15

*In which Ophelia
has a feeling*

———◆———

So there it was. Alice's words rang inside Ophelia's ears and made her cheeks burn. She wiped angrily at the tears that kept wanting to appear when they had no right. Alice had changed. She'd been changing for months, but now it was as though the process had hastened. Alice was freezing; her heart was freezing. That's the only way Ophelia could think to describe it.

Alice doesn't mean it, said her mother in her ear. *She's not herself.*

"Don't make excuses for her," said Ophelia aloud.

She went back down the stairs, slowly this time. Gathering her strength. She opened her map, looked at it, crumpled it into a ball, and threw it in the nearest garbage receptacle.

She turned and ran back up the stairs again. She ran back up the stairs like someone about to miss a bus. She ran back up furiously, and the gallery of dresses was gone. In its place was the small silver elevator that would take her to the sixth floor.

"I knew it," Ophelia said.

This time she was prepared for the polar bear. She sped past the flags of the world, the artwork stacked in teetering heaps, the mountain of sewing machines, and the several stuffed parrots.

Parrots! She stopped still. It had changed back again. She looked for the windows and the carriage, but they were nowhere to be seen. There was the anchor, and there was the locomotive, and there was the pile of jewelry boxes.

"Boy," she said, and the word echoed in the silence.

But she knew she wouldn't be able to find him.

"Where are you?"

The merry-go-round horses watched her with their glossy, sad eyes.

But there was no reply at all.

Ophelia left the sixth floor and returned to where the corridors were filling with people. She moved through the crowds. They were waiting in snake lines at the entrances to galleries. They were peering into display cabinets; at brains floating in yellowish liquid; at medical devices, sharp and silvery; at rabbits' feet amulets and ivory lockets and four-leaf clovers, hundreds of them inside smudgy glass cases.

Near the *Gallery of Time* the crowd was surging. It was moving one step forward and two steps back as people tried to push their way in to get the best view. The guards were shouting.

"Move back!" they yelled. "There is space for all. Micro-phones have been placed near the clock. You will hear it chime everywhere."

And indeed the ticking of the clock was magnified. It was everywhere in the corridors, like a dreadful heartbeat.

Where would they put the boy? Where would they hide him?

She rushed first to his room, 303, but the door was open there, the room swept clean. She had to find the boy, she just had to. Wherever they had hidden him, she hoped he was warm. He had nothing but that old, thin coat.

She raced through rooms, pushing against the tide of the crowd. Through a room filled with buttons. A room filled with beetles. A large, circular room with a dome-shaped roof, filled with nothing but broken toys. Jack-in-the-boxes that wouldn't jump, dolls without legs, teddy bears without stuffing, and dollhouses, all of them empty, without a single stitch of furni-ture. Ophelia shivered in that place.

Oh my, her mother whispered in her ear.

"I knew you'd like it," said Ophelia angrily.

Think, said her mother. *Where haven't you been yet?*

She knew what her mother was going to say. She was going to say, *You haven't been to the seventh floor, to the right-hand cor-ridor to the Queen's chambers.*

"Don't even say it," said Ophelia. "What about the gardens? On the map there was a Winter Garden. And I saw a sign for it near the refectory. Perhaps they've put him outside. I have a . . . feeling."

A feeling! She hated saying that. Psychics had feelings. Fortune-tellers and clairvoyants had feelings. Not amateur scientists from the Children's Science Society of Greater London.

But she couldn't ignore the feeling, the feeling that the boy was cold. There, she'd said it. That thought made her heart hurt.

"It's his stockings. They're full of holes. Oh, I can't explain it," said Ophelia.

I understand, whispered her mother.

Ophelia could feel her smiling beside her ear. She pulled down on her braids.

The Winter Garden, then, whispered her mother as Ophelia began to run.

She went past the pavilion of wolves and stared through the pillars at them. They didn't move. They didn't breathe. Down corridors and up staircases and down again. Through the refectory to where a very faded sign above a stairwell pointed to PREHISTORIA and the ROYAL WINTER GARDEN.

The stairwell was very dim, and *Prehistoria* was even dimmer. It was filled up with nothing but rock and stone, bones laid out in grimy display cabinets and skulls all in a line. Someone had left their bag of chips there right in among them. And at the very back of *Prehistoria*, there was a very nondescript door with the words WINTER GARDEN written in very small letters—only the *G* had been lost, and she found it down on the ground. She felt the handle. It was stiff with age, but it turned. And Ophelia stepped from the museum into the outside.

16

*In which Ophelia
finds a Herald Tree*

———◆———

There was something about the outside that made Ophelia want to cry. Perhaps it was the snow. Perhaps all the trees, or the skeletons of the trees, with their spindly arms raised to the white sky. Or the statues, statue after statue, standing motionless. There were girls dancing and boys with arrows aimed at the clouds. Perhaps it was their stillness that made her feel so bad.

Perhaps she should go inside.

Perhaps she should give up.

She could turn and walk back inside. She could find her father.

She could say, "I'm sorry, I've been so silly. I feel better now. We aren't in danger at all. Tonight the Wintertide Clock will chime, and there will be an exhibition about swords. The world will not end. The boy was all in my imagination. I never knew my imagination was good. I think it's all the snow."

These were terrible thoughts.

Treacherous.

Even her mother gasped in her ear.

You should never give up on a disappearing boy, her mother whispered, *not ever. Disappearing boys need friends; it's the only thing keeping them alive.*

"Yes," said Ophelia as she kept walking. "Yes, I know."

It began to snow heavily, falling in drifts. All Ophelia could see were the outlines of walls and the shapes of what might have been low hedges, now white. She shuffled through the snow. There were stone creatures, she noticed, covered in frost. Eagles with outstretched wings and lions reclining on the walls and a white horse rising up on its hind legs as though startled, only frozen now in time.

More leafless trees, an avenue of them, glittering with ice.

He could never survive outside here. Never.

Ophelia's chest felt very tight. She took her puffer from her newly sewn pocket and puffed twice. The thing about the boy was that she missed him. She missed him so much. Just thinking of him captured, locked up somewhere anew. The Queen, planning to . . .

The trouble with magic was that it was messy and dangerous and filled with longing. There were too many moments that made your heart stop and ache and start again.

She looked for doors. Doors that might lead into small walled gardens. Perhaps he was locked away inside one. In an outdoor pavilion. She ran her finger along the walls, feeling for seams, the edges of a door. The snow made her gloves wet, and her fingers stung.

The problem with magic was that it made her feel very alone.

She knew the boy was true. He was as real as she was. And she had to save him.

And in thinking these things, she felt her finger hit something on the wall. A fine edge. She stopped and started to scrape away the ice and snow, and it wasn't long before she realized that it was the outline of a little recessed iron door. She carefully scraped away the snow hanging from the door handle. Then she turned the handle, holding her breath, waiting to see what lay behind.

The boy was not in the walled garden. In the walled garden there was a tree. The tree had a plump trunk and a spreading canopy of branches, but it was probably only twice as tall as Ophelia. It was a pleasant tree. She imagined in spring it might have very deep green leaves, and one could lie beneath it in the shade. A soothing, calming kind of tree. A lazing-beneath-it kind of tree. The branches shone with ice, however, and there was not one single hint of greenery in that tiny walled garden.

Ophelia looked around the tree, at the ground. She kicked at snow. She felt with her feet for the hidden sword, just in case. She knew it wasn't there. Her feeling had brought her here, and here was the Herald Tree.

Here was the Herald Tree that the boy had spoken of.

She had tried to ignore it, but here it was.

She knelt down in the snow, quite close to it. Timidly held out her hand. Of course she wouldn't be able to hear anything, would she? It wasn't like she was magical in any way. She hadn't been trained by the wizards. She didn't know how to do it.

She placed her hand flat against the cold trunk.

It won't hurt to try, whispered her mother. *It never hurts to try.*

Ophelia Jane Worthington-Whittard closed her eyes.

Later she would say it was like being plugged into an electrical socket. When she touched the Herald Tree, she felt something bright enter her. She tingled in her toes, and her glasses thrummed against her face, and she felt her braids lift, just a little, from her shoulders.

She heard several things at once. Footsteps on a winding wooden staircase, robes rustling, someone singing, and another sound like fingers kneading dough. And all these things she heard as though they were going on right inside of her: as though the staircase were there in her body, and the dough were being kneaded inside her tummy, and someone were singing quietly inside her lungs.

Ophelia, said a voice.

The voice was very deep and very low, and it reminded her of velvet and rolling waves. The voice came from the tree and into her fingers and into her blood, and she felt her name move up her arm and into her heart.

"How do you know me?" Ophelia didn't know if she spoke those words or those words spoke her.

We have always known you.

"That doesn't make sense."

It will soon.

"I can't find the sword. I've looked everywhere."

The sword will find you.

"How?"

You are a girl of many questions, as prophesied.

Ophelia had never been prophesied before. It made her feel annoyed.

"I rescued the boy, but then the Queen's taken him again. She's hidden him somewhere new. Now I have to find him along with everything else."

You will find him, said the voice. *We have seen it. It has all been told.*

You're all very sure, Ophelia wanted to say but didn't, though the wizards heard her anyway.

She heard one laugh, a deep belly laugh.

All will be well in the end, Ophelia, the voices said in unison.

And that reminded her of something, although she couldn't say what. She felt the seal between her hand and the tree weaken and her braids land on her back and her shoulders slump forward, and she was released from the current of the Herald Tree.

She stood up and dusted off her knees, not sure at all what to do, except she noticed she had started to cry—tears were flowing down her cheeks and turning to ice as they went. She scrunched her fists up in her eyes and stamped her feet on the ground. Her tears cracked and tinkled and fell to the ground, and she didn't try to stop them for some time.

* * *

Wizards, she thought, when she gained her composure. What good were they if they couldn't tell you how to do stuff, if they were always talking in riddles and saying they knew everything before it even happened? It wasn't very helpful.

If she were a wizard, she'd write reports for people. She'd make sure everything was very clear. She'd write, *Looking for a magical sword? No problem. Go to the fifth floor, turn left, open a large wooden chest, et cetera, et cetera.* She'd have check boxes. *Found your magical sword? Place X here.*

She went back inside the museum, her breath smoking before her in great clouds. She dusted away the rest of her frozen tears. She walked through the darkened *Prehistoria* and then entered an elevator to find her way back to her father's workroom. Following her heart had got her nowhere. She needed a plan. She'd go to her father. She'd say, "I've had a nap; I'm feeling much better. Can I go through your lists of swords? Your spreadsheets? It's very important."

She went on tiptoe across the sea monster mosaic. She hoped she wouldn't meet the horrible Mr. Pushkinova again. She checked again in room 303, but the boy wasn't there. The door in the turquoise sea was still open, and the bed had been stripped bare. The floor had been scrubbed, and the pitcher and porridge bowl cleaned and turned upside down on the table.

It made her feel abandoned. Yes, that was the word.

She went back out through the stone angels and across the sea monster mosaic and down the long, thin gallery of painted girls in party dresses.

"Hello, Tess Janson," she said. "You're looking very bored.

Hello, Katie Patin, Matilda Cole, Johanna Payne, Judith Pickford, Millie Mayfield, Carys Sprock, Sally Temple-Watts, Paulette Claude, and Kyra Marinova."

She stopped there. Put her hand up to touch Kyra's face, even though she knew you should never touch paintings in a museum.

She moved to the next painting.

"Hello, Alice Worthington-Whittard," she said.

She stopped.

She opened her mouth.

She tried to comprehend.

A hundred thoughts swarmed into her head, buzzed madly, swarmed out again. Alice. Painted. Chosen by the Queen. Miss Kaminski. The seventh floor . . . *the machine.*

17

In which Ophelia must rescue her sister, Alice

———◆———

She tried, with all her might, not to think of the misery birds. As she went up in the elevator, she tried to think of boys' names beginning with *F* instead. She couldn't think of many of those. There were just Fabien, Finnigan, Falstaff, Fred, Felix, Fergus, and Floyd.

They'd be waiting on their roosts, listening, those misery birds.

Gerald, Greg, Geronimo, Gus, Gulliver, Grant, Gabriel, Galahad, Gavin.

They hadn't eaten for one whole day, those misery birds. They'd be ravenous.

She'd said she'd never come again to the seventh floor, and here she was. She had to save Alice. And she was sure this was where Alice was.

It's the right thing to do, whispered her mother.

"But it's scary," Ophelia whispered back.

You'll rescue Alice, and then you can look for the sword while you're there as well. And the satchel and compass and the instructions the wizards gave the boy. Those are sure to help.

As though Ophelia were only doing something simple, like shopping.

"It's all right for you," said Ophelia.

She remembered quite suddenly the morning she didn't hear her mother's footsteps on the stairs outside her bedroom. The loose floorboard didn't creak. She didn't hear the study door open nor the chair squeak. She didn't hear her mother's fingers flying on the keyboard. Everything was still.

That morning Ophelia slipped out of bed and walked across the hall and up the stairs. She paused outside her parents' bedroom. There was another noise.

Smaller.

Scratchier.

She pushed the door open. Her father was on his side, fast asleep. Her mother was propped up on her pillows, a notebook open in her lap. She was writing with a pencil.

"I thought . . . ," said Ophelia. The sense of relief had made her feel dizzy.

"I'm still here," said her mother.

Ophelia waited for the elevator door to clang open on the seventh floor. She stood in the silence that followed, her legs shaking. She began to walk very quietly across the marble floor, for the first time toward the right-hand corridor. There were no rooms in this corridor, just bare white walls, and in the distance—it seemed forever away—one single door. Ophelia walked toward it. There was a tiny plaque on the door. She could see it from a distance but could not make out the words. When she was closer, she adjusted her glasses. She didn't want to read the words. She was terrified of what she would see.

The plaque read in small silver letters:

MISS KAMINSKI

MUSEUM CURATOR

I knew she was bad from the beginning, her mother hissed.

"Shh," said Ophelia.

She knocked very quietly on the door, and when no one answered, she opened it.

"Alice," she whispered.

There was no reply.

It was a very plain office. There was an old white sofa and an old pine box that served as a coffee table. An old bookshelf. The walls and curtains were white, and the desk was also a pale pine. There was one large crystal paperweight holding down a thin pile of papers. Behind the desk, a window gave a view of the cold city.

Ophelia took a puff on her inhaler, and she wished she hadn't because it was a very loud noise in the very quiet room. She started with the desk. She lifted up the paperweight first and went through the small pile of papers beneath. Seating arrangements. All of them written by hand in a silvery ink.

In the first drawer, there was a silver pen. In the second drawer, white sheets of writing paper. In the third drawer, there

194

was nothing but a frosted pink lipstick, a hand mirror, and a packet of mints. In the fourth drawer, there was a silver key.

Ophelia ran her fingers along the spines of the books in Miss Kaminski's bookshelf. *Prehistoric Art. The Amulets of Eastern Europe. The Museum in the Late Twentieth Century. Franco-Flemish Social History.* She sat down on the sofa and looked at the pine-box coffee table. She saw that the box had a lock. She went back to the desk and retrieved the key.

The box was stiff with age, but the key opened it. The lid made a hideous squeak. Inside was the satchel, worn smooth by time. She opened it, and she took out the folded piece of paper. It was a little crumpled. A little stained. A fragile, ancient thing. And written in the Great Wizard's strange block letters on the outside, the word *Instructions*.

She felt in the bag again.

There it was, the old, tarnished compass. She held it in her hand before placing it back inside. Her fingers brushed against something else. She peered inside and saw a little biscuit man, two shiny currant eyes staring back at her. She slipped the satchel strap over her head and shoulder, and it fitted perfectly.

"Oh, Alice, where are you?" Ophelia said into the quiet room.

Sitting there on the sofa, she became aware of a very faint vibration through the soles of her feet. She stood up. When she moved toward the door, it grew weaker. If she moved toward the bookshelf, it grew stronger.

"Alice," Ophelia whispered into the quiet. "Alice."

Nothing.

She touched the bookshelf, and it thrummed beneath her fingertips. Something was behind it. She felt with her fingers. She felt the shelves and the spines of the books. Perhaps there was a secret switch. She lifted the books forward one by one, starting at the bottom right-hand corner. She nearly gave up. But Ophelia Jane Worthington-Whittard was always very thorough.

The very last book, in the top left-hand corner, opened the door.

The bookshelf slid to one side, and the secret room was revealed.

Ophelia gasped with astonishment.

"Alice!" she shouted.

The machine was in the center of the small, secret room. It was a dull gray color, about the size and shape of a coffin. It hummed and gurgled and vibrated violently as Ophelia rushed around it, looking for a way to stop it.

At the very end there was a large black lever. Ophelia pulled down hard on it, with all her might, but felt her feet lift from the ground from her exertion.

"I'm trying, Alice!" she shouted. "I'll get you out of there."

She tried again and again, jumped and pushed down, cried out with her efforts until finally she felt the lever give, and the machine's violent droning ceased. The lid hissed open and lying there, perfect, more beautiful than she had ever seen her, was Alice.

18

*In which it becomes apparent that
Alice has broken the machine*

———◆———

Alice opened her blue eyes. She stared angrily at Ophelia. "What'd you do that for?" she said. "I don't think you're meant to stop it. You shouldn't interrupt beauty treatments."

She sat up scowling and swung her legs over the side. "Do I look all right?" she asked.

"That isn't a beauty treatment," said Ophelia. "I've just rescued you. Who put you in there?"

"Miss Kaminski, of course. Why?"

"I knew it. That machine was going to extract your soul and turn you into a ghost," said Ophelia. "Then you'd be trapped forever in the forest, and the Snow Queen—Miss Kaminski—would be stronger and live forever."

"Are you insane, Ophelia?" asked Alice as she rummaged in her handbag for her mirror. "Miss Kaminski said the machine would improve my skin and make me look more beautiful than ever."

Ophelia shook her head. "It's true, Alice. Think about it: why would she put you in this thing, in a hidden room, at the very top of the museum. Why?"

"It was a little strange, I thought," said Alice.

"Of course it's strange."

"And it did seem weird when she laughed after she closed the lid."

"There!" said Ophelia. "She's pure evil."

"But she said she'd come back in an hour to get me."

"Alice, think about it," said Ophelia, but she could tell she was losing Alice.

Her sister touched her hair, and with a flick of her head, shook away her suspicions. "She said it was all very safe."

"It's not safe, Alice," Ophelia said. "And I'm not insane. Terrible things are happening here. When the Wintertide Clock chimes, the world will end."

Ophelia was aware of how it sounded.

"Do you know what time it is, then?" asked Alice. She was back to looking at herself. She touched her cheeks. "I think the beauty treatment has made a difference."

"It's just after four," said Ophelia, looking at her watch. Their mother had been gone three months, nine days, and fifteen hours.

"Four! I'm meant to be at the sword exhibition hall by four," said Alice. "They'll be waiting for me."

"I can't believe you broke the machine," said Ophelia.

"What did you say?" said Alice, but she didn't wait for an answer. She was quickly applying lipstick. "And what's that hideous bag you've got on?"

"It's a special bag. It has a message from a wizard and a magic compass and a biscuit."

"Ophelia, you're *so* weird," said Alice, rushing past her, running her hands through her hair, her crystal dress sweeping behind her.

19

*In which Ophelia reads
the wizard's instructions*

———◆———

The amplified ticking of the Wintertide Clock was very loud in the galleries and the corridors. The sound reached every inch of the museum; it filled every small space and every large dazzling room. It beat and beat and beat, and Ophelia felt it in her stomach and in her toes. It was a countdown. A countdown to the end. It was the ticking of a time bomb. And nobody knew.

She would find her father. She'd have to make him understand.

Ophelia Jane Worthington-Whittard raced through *Oriental Tapestries*, *Neolithic Man*, *Alchemy: The Exhibition*. She took the clanking elevator to the *Age of Enlightenment*. As she ran, she glanced everywhere for the sword.

She went through a small room containing a collection of Chinese finger bowls, another containing medieval jewelry. She ran through a re-creation of a nineteenth-century street.

When she'd found her father, she'd say, "Dad, stop. Stop what you are doing. You have to stop and understand."

She sped past a small collection of fossils, *Farming Equipment, Culture of the Cossacks*, dolls, teddy bears, shoes, *History of Silhouettes* (which she was sure was in a different place now). There were rocks, gemstones, a room filled floor to ceiling with sepia photographs. There were *Romans at Work* and *Romans at Leisure*.

Ophelia, said her mother. *Slow down. Think about what you have with you.*

She slowed down. She stopped in a very big space filled with several stuffed elephants, their saddles and headdresses studded with jewels.

"What do I have?" said Ophelia aloud. "I have nothing. I can't find the boy. I can't find the sword. I haven't even started to look for the One Other."

Breathe, said her mother, very calmly. *Find a place to sit down.*

Ophelia walked to a window behind the elephants. She felt her stomach growl. How long since she had eaten? She saw the sky had grown dim. The streetlights had come on. The snow whirled and spiraled to the ground. Her body ached with tiredness.

You have the boy's satchel, don't you? asked her mother.

Ophelia opened the satchel. She took out the little biscuit man Petal had baked all those years ago. If she ate it, perhaps it would give her the strength to keep going? She raised the magical biscuit man to her mouth and then stopped. Her mouth watered, but she put the biscuit man back into the satchel. She knew it wasn't meant for her.

Instead she took out the fragile paper containing the words from the Great Wizard. She unfolded the thin piece of paper.

The letter was written in a very old-fashioned writing, a little shaky. It was a list.

First, always be kind, it read.

Be kind to everyone whom you meet along the way, and things will be well.

Kindness is far stronger than any cruelty.

Always extend your hand in friendship.

Be patient.

You may feel alone, but there will always be people who will help you along the way.

Never, ever give up.

Ophelia leaned her cheek against the cold window. She closed her eyes.

Your heart, said her mother, very softly in her ear. *Use your heart, my dear daughter.*

20

In which Ophelia remembers some other words and an owl in a tree

———◆———

A t the end Susan Worthington liked to rest in a chair in the front sitting room, in the sunshine. The sitting room had comfortable chairs and a cuckoo clock, which they had bought in Switzerland, and family photographs on the walls: Alice and Ophelia smiling beside the sea, buckets in hand. Alice as a baby in her mother's arms. Susan and Malcolm on their wedding day. It was a good room, bright and warm and full of love.

One day her mother had called Ophelia there.

"Come here, let me clean your glasses," her mother said. She cleaned them with the hem of her skirt. "There, you should always do that. Promise me you'll do that at least three times a day."

Her mother had grown very thin. Her hands were bony and pale. Her hair had grown back in small tufts. That day she had a deep blue scarf on her head.

"You look tired," she said to Ophelia.

"There's this owl," said Ophelia. "It has been hooting every night in the tree in the front garden."

"I've heard it too," said her mother.

"And once I got up to look out the window, and I could see its big golden eyes shining in the dark."

"I wish I'd seen that."

"You could put it in one of your books."

"I just might," her mother replied. "Come here. One of your ponytails is higher than the other."

"That always happens," said Ophelia, "when I have to do it myself."

"You'll get better at it," said her mother.

She smoothed back Ophelia's bangs and straightened her school tie. "I want to talk to you."

"What about?"

"About everything."

"I don't want to talk about it," said Ophelia, because she knew what her mother wanted to say.

"When I'm gone, you mustn't be terribly sad," said her mother.

"Don't say that."

"I'm only telling you in case," said her mother. "Promise me you won't stay too sad forever."

"Don't talk about it," said Ophelia. She put her hands over her ears.

"Ophelia, darling. Listen. I want to talk to you." She took Ophelia's hands from her ears.

It was a perfectly ordinary day when they had that conversation. The mail thumped through the mailbox onto the foyer tiles. A truck started up somewhere outside. There was a gaggle of schoolgirls passing outside on the street, shrieking with laughter.

"Sit on my lap," said her mother. "Like you did when you were a little girl."

She sat on her mother's lap, and they didn't say anything. The clock tick, tick, ticked. She lay against her mother's chest and listened to her heart beat.

"I just wanted to tell you that everything will be well," said her mother, "in the end."

"When will I know it's the end?" asked Ophelia.

"I will write it for you," said her mother.

"In capitals?"

"In capitals."

"With a full stop?"

"With a full stop."

"Underlined?"

"Underlined."

21

In which Ophelia uses her heart,
and the compass comes in handy

———◆———

Ophelia Jane Worthington-Whittard liked to think scientifically, but that hadn't worked. She knew her mother was right. She knew there was no point in looking for evidence or compiling lists, shading maps, or asking questions. But if it was her heart she had to trust, then why wasn't her heart speaking to her?

You have to stop thinking so much, whispered her mother.

Which was much more difficult to do than to say.

Look in the satchel again, whispered her mother.

Ophelia opened the satchel again and peered inside. She saw something glinting, and when her hands closed around it, she found it was the compass. She took it and held it flat in the palm of her hand. It was very old and tarnished, and the arrow swung wildly as she turned it from side to side. She'd done orienteering once with her class. They'd been given a list of certain things they had to find and a map with coordinates.

Lucy Coutts had won, of course. She won everything, or nearly everything, and if she didn't win, she turned red and became very cross.

What had the wizards told the boy? Always make sure that the compass points south. Ophelia held the compass and turned until she found south. It was just an idea. Only an idea. But the idea gave her butterflies, and the butterflies danced in her stomach. Take me to the sword, then, she thought. Yes, that sounded like her heart speaking.

"Take me to the sword," she said aloud.

Ophelia followed south. South took her down two flights of stairs with malachite banisters, which she had never seen before. South took her through the pavilion of wolves, past the elephants again, straight through the *Gallery of Time*, which was very difficult because of the crowd. The crowd pressed against her. She weaved her way under arms and legs, crawled the last section on the floor along a wall.

South took her into a silvery elevator and out the other side, down the stairwell to the sword workroom, which made her briefly excited, until she was there and found it was almost completely empty. She followed south to the very back of the room, where there was another door that led to a storage space: a jumble of cardboard boxes and plastic that had been torn from mannequins, and even a mannequin too, which hadn't been used, lying on his side, with his doll eyes staring straight ahead forlornly.

Ophelia's father appeared from the back of the storeroom.

"There you are!" he said. "I tried to phone you and Alice at the hotel. Then I saw Alice in the gallery, and she said you were resting here. I was very worried you'd run off again."

Now, why would the compass lead Ophelia to her father?

Her heart sank. She tried not to look disappointed. But she felt tears smart in her eyes. It was just an idea. A stupid idea. Of course the compass wouldn't take her to the sword. Of course not. Of course she couldn't save the world.

"And you're meant to be resting, darling. Look at you. You are still looking very peaky."

The tears spilled over her eyelids. She tried to stifle a sob. Of course, she thought, of course. There was no hope for anything. She'd be frozen soon. It wouldn't matter. Everyone would be . . . finished.

"Darling, what's wrong? Why are you crying? What have you got in your hand there?"

Ophelia clutched the compass to herself and fell into his arms.

Her father, who was not very good yet at embracing or at wiping away tears, put his arms around her. "It's okay, Ophelia," he said. "Whatever's wrong, it's okay."

"It's not okay," she sobbed. "It's not. I'm not okay, and you're not okay, and Alice is not okay. It's no good pretending that it is."

"Ophelia," said her father. He took a handkerchief from his pocket to try to dry her eyes.

"No," she said. "You can't just keep pretending it's all fine. We're sad. We're all so sad."

"It's okay to be sad," said her father.

"Then why don't you ever show it? Why won't you ever talk about her?" she cried, pulling away from him.

Mr. Whittard looked dreadful then. He clenched his jaw, and tears appeared in his eyes. He shook his head. "I'm sorry," he said. "I'm sorry. I'm trying as hard as I can."

"I want her back," said Ophelia.

"I want her back too," said her father, beginning to sob.

Ophelia embraced her father hard until she felt him embrace her in return. She took the handkerchief and wiped the tears slowly from his eyes.

"I've just remembered something," he said finally. "I found something this afternoon that I know will cheer us up."

"What?" Ophelia said, wiping her eyes.

"Come with me." He led her further inside the storage area, to the very back of the small room. "It isn't much to look at, I know. But it does look very old, and it has a carving that could be a closed eye. There was no place for it in the show, of course. I'm actually thinking, at one stage, it may have been a toy, although a rather heavy one."

He bent down into a pile of broken stuff, which had been pushed into a far corner of the room. He rummaged around.

"Here it is," he said.

He handed the sword to Ophelia. The strange, rather ugly-looking sword. The sword with the smooth wooden hilt and the tarnished blade. She held it in her hands. She didn't say a word. The eye opened just above the blade. A green gem showed.

"I never noticed that there before," said her father.

She felt the sword singing and humming in her hands. It felt as light as air. As though it had a life of its own. She slashed with it in front of her suddenly.

"Hold on one minute," said her father. "Be careful. I need to look at that thing again; I never saw that stone before. . . ."

But Ophelia wasn't handing it over. She laughed. Already the tears were drying on her face. "Daddy," she said. "I love you. Do you know the time?"

"It's half past five," Mr. Whittard said. "Where are you going?"

She was running out of the room as fast as she could, with the sword raised before her. She called back to her father. "I'll be back soon. I've just got to save the world."

Ophelia didn't know where the boy was, but she ran as though she could find him in time. She pushed through the crowd that had entered through the museum foyer. They came in waves through the great revolving doors, and the snow came with them. It was like trying to swim upstream. She was pushed and pulled, and once she fell and only barely moved out of the way of a boot.

There was no point in trying the elevators. People were jamming themselves inside, and the guards were shouting and banging them over the heads with their handbags. She took the grand staircase two steps at a time. She ran with the sword in her hand and her two braids streaming behind her. She took her puffer from her pocket and squirted as she went.

The sword took her. That was what she said afterward. It

flew in front of her with a life of its own, and all she had to do was try to keep up. People scowled at her. People jumped out of the way. People called out for the guards.

Some thought it was part of the exhibition and applauded as she passed.

Then the crowd petered out in the dimmer parts of the museum. Past the gallery of teaspoons and the shadowy arcade of mirrors and down the long, gloomy gallery of painted girls. She ran as though just the act of running alone would take her to him.

The dinosaur hall was far from the crowds, and when she hit the elevator button, she heard it rumbling from above. With the sword in her hands, she didn't feel frightened. Well, only a little. She slashed it in front of her, and it sang a song. She stepped inside the elevator and pressed floor 7. The boy must be somewhere on the seventh floor. He must. The elevator began to move, complaining and whining upward, but it stopped suddenly on only the third floor. The doors opened, and all of Ophelia's bravery evaporated. There before her stood Mr. Pushkinova.

22

*In which Ophelia has a conversation
with Mr. Pushkinova*

———◆———

Ophelia lunged toward the CLOSE button, but Mr. Push-kinova, rather casually, put his hand between the doors. He said nothing. He snarled. A low, grumbling snarl. Ophelia raised the sword at him. He looked a little worried at that, but still he stepped inside the elevator with her. The doors closed behind him. The elevator began to travel upward.

"I—I—I need to know where the boy is," stammered Ophelia, pointing the sword at Mr. Pushkinova.

"There is nothing you can do to help him," he whispered.

"But look, I've found the sword," said Ophelia. "That's all he needs."

He moved toward her, and she jabbed at him. He seemed surprised. The sword made a noise like a hissing cat.

The elevator went on up, up, up. It didn't seem possible that it could keep going.

"He said you were good," said Ophelia. "He said you were a very good man."

Mr. Pushkinova hesitated.

"I don't believe him; I didn't believe him. But I'm not so sure. Why would he say you were good if you weren't? He knows everything there is to know about good and bad."

Mr. Pushkinova snarled. But it was halfhearted.

"He said you were his friend," Ophelia continued.

"There is nothing you can do to help him," Mr. Pushkinova repeated, although this time his voice shook. He closed his eyes as though he were trying to erase the boy from his memory. And from his heart.

"All these years of you taking him his porridge and talking to him."

Mr. Pushkinova said nothing.

"Please," said Ophelia.

At last the old man opened his eyes. "I have told you twice, little girl. There is nothing that you can do. What can you do against the force of winter? Have you thought of that? What can you do? Can you not imagine the strength of the Queen?"

"But if you've looked after him all these years, how can you not care about him?"

"He has been a good boy," said Mr. Pushkinova. "In the beginning he ran away often but never got far. He was full of spirit in those days. Always, every day, hoping for the person who would rescue him. The one that the wizards had told him of. He pinned all his hopes on this. And look. Now we are at the very end, and this person has not arrived."

Two tears slipped from Ophelia's eyes.

"But I never even got to say goodbye to him," said Ophelia. "And he's my friend."

Mr. Pushkinova sighed. "He's not up here," he said.

"Where?"

"He is laid out in the Winter Garden."

"But I've been to the Winter Garden. I didn't see him."

"You will find him there. He is waiting. . . ."

"Waiting for what?"

"Use your imagination, child," said Mr. Pushkinova, but he said it very sadly.

His shoulders slumped, he leaned back against the doors, and he pressed the button for down.

"He said you were good," whispered Ophelia. "He said all these years you have been his only friend. He would like you to know that."

"He is in the Winter Garden," Mr. Pushkinova said. The door opened in *Prehistoria*. "But there will be nothing you can do to save him, child."

23

*In which Ophelia finds both
the boy and the One Other*

———◆———

I t was terrible to think of him being outside. He would
be freezing in just his golden coat and his stockings and
knickerbockers, without a scarf or a hat or even gloves. She ran
out into the courtyard and found that the snow had stopped
briefly, but also that it was so chilled that it took her breath
away. It was perfectly still, and the world was perfectly glittering and shining, like a Christmas bauble.

"Boy!" she shouted into the white landscape.

"Take me to him!" she shouted to the sword, and it pulled
at her arms like a dog on a leash, and she skidded and skated
across the ice, her braids streaming behind her.

The sword did not enter the walled garden but rather the
large open space of the courtyard. There were statues there as
well. Giant ones, covered in snow, so that it was impossible to
tell anymore what they might be. She rushed past their shadows, drawn by the sword.

"Good sword," she said. "Good sword."

The sword took her to the very center of the courtyard and stopped her there. There was nothing but a mound of snow. It was a mound of snow like a mound of earth on a freshly filled grave. Ophelia squeaked. The sword fell from her hands. She knelt down and began to dig as fast as she could. She dug furiously, tears spilling from her eyes, the air squeezed from her chest by the cold.

"Please, please, please," she said. And her fingers hit something cold and hard. She wiped at the thing frantically and uncovered the Marvelous Boy's face, which was marble white, his eyebrows frosted, his lips blue. She sat in the snow beside him, crying and trying to loosen the ties that held him there.

He opened his eyes, and Ophelia cried out in astonishment.

"Ophelia," he said. "I knew you would come."

"Look, I found it," she said, holding up the sword.

"I knew you would."

She worked at the ties, her fingers numb. The Marvelous Boy tried to sit up, but he was very weak. She helped him. She took his hand between hers and blew on it.

"Miss Kaminski is the Snow Queen," she said. "Alice nearly got her soul extracted in the machine, but I got her out. I nearly gave up, but then my father—it was my father who found the sword. But I still don't know who I am meant to give it to."

The Marvelous Boy took the sword. In his hands it was heavy again. He could barely lift it. He was very faded. The three-hundred-and-three-year-old boy. Ophelia could almost see straight through him.

"I will be going soon," he said.

"Please don't go," she said. She wrapped her arms around his neck.

He embraced her in return. "Ophelia Jane Worthington-Whittard," he said. "Do you not know what the great magical owl whispered into my ear that day?"

Ophelia was confused.

"The name he whispered," said the Marvelous Boy. "That name was Ophelia."

He tried to hand the sword to her.

"Don't be silly," said Ophelia. "It couldn't be me."

"The sword is yours," he said.

"Don't be silly," said Ophelia again.

"I'm not," he said. "It really is yours."

He took one of her hands and placed the sword there. "Do you not feel it?"

"But I don't know what to do with it," Ophelia cried, and wiped her nose with her other hand.

There was the green eye again, as soon as she held the sword.

"Ophelia Jane Worthington-Whittard," the boy said again. He held his hand over her hand on the sword.

"Don't," she said, and began to cry more.

"I invest in you," he said, "the power to be the defender of goodness and happiness and hope."

So she stood up and held the sword, which sang and rattled magic in her hands, and turned to see the Snow Queen coming across the courtyard.

24

In which a great battle takes place

The Snow Queen strode across the courtyard. She laughed and shook her head at the sight of Ophelia and the Marvelous Boy. She wore a white satin dress and a dazzling crown on her head. She raised the Great Sorrow, and the snow swirled around her feet. A path was cleared before her in the snow as she walked. She was oblivious to the cold.

"You're too late," said the Marvelous Boy when she was near. "The sword now belongs to the One Other."

The Snow Queen laughed even more at that. "What do you think this little weed will be able to do?"

Ophelia held the sword. It jerked this way and that in her hands.

The Queen came toward the boy slowly. She smiled sweetly, then thrust the Great Sorrow toward him until it was inches from his chest. "Soon. Five minutes more and you're gone," she said.

The Marvelous Boy shivered but smiled.

"And you," said the Snow Queen, pointing the sword at Ophelia. "You are not long for this world either."

Ophelia tried to hold the magical sword still before her, but it leapt and slashed toward the Snow Queen. It lunged forward in her hands, and Ophelia flew behind it. The Snow Queen was ready—she struck out with her own sword, and the two clashed.

"You cannot defeat me. I will reign supreme," said the Queen, and the sword in Ophelia's hands leapt again. The Snow Queen parried, but this time the weight of Ophelia's thrust knocked her to the ground.

"Sorry," said Ophelia, and drew the sword back with all her might.

"A mistake," said the Queen, laughing, and she was up on her feet again in a single motion.

"Ophelia!" shouted a voice, and she turned to see her father running through the snow. He was carrying a Spanish long sword, and she knew it was not one he would have chosen if he hadn't been in a rush.

"Miss Kaminski!" her father shouted as he raced toward them. "We saw you from the window in the sword hall. What are you both doing out here? Why are you pointing a sword at my daughter?"

The Snow Queen lunged suddenly at Ophelia, who fell back onto her bottom in the snow.

"Leave my sister alone!" shouted Alice, who had followed her father into the courtyard. "I don't understand."

The Snow Queen looked at Alice, this time with momentary confusion. How could the girl be out of the machine?

"Stop it this instant, Miss Kaminski!" shouted Mr. Whittard. He raised his sword. "I've no idea what you're doing, but it isn't right. Please put down your sword and come inside."

"Oh really," said the Snow Queen. "You are all very amusing."

She raised her sword and walked toward Mr. Whittard. She slashed it in the air in front of him.

He fought back.

"What on earth is going on?" he exclaimed. He looked to Ophelia for some sort of clue.

"I've been trying to tell you, Daddy," cried Ophelia.

The Snow Queen thrust toward Mr. Whittard. He lunged forward in a sleek and dashing move. The two swords met and then fell apart again.

They clashed and clanged across the courtyard, the Snow Queen stalking him in her stilettos.

"Who do you think you are?" she whispered.

"Pardon?" said Mr. Whittard.

"I said, who do you think you are?" screamed the Snow Queen.

"I think the question is rather *Who* are *you?*" said Mr. Whittard.

The Snow Queen shouted something in her own language. Something magical, from her sad place of frost and snow.

"I'll show you," she said.

* * *

In the *Gallery of Time* the hands of the Wintertide Clock moved to 6 p.m. The clock chimed. The chime was beautiful and terrible at the same time. The bells rang out a cascading song of sadness. Those who heard it said it was like glass breaking, others attested it was the sound of tears. Some said it was like a wind crying, and others said that it was like the falling of snow.

The little gilt door in the clock's face opened, and out came a chill wisp of wind. It wound its way out of the room and into the corridors. It froze dawdlers who had not made it to the sword exhibition hall—it froze them exactly where they stood.

In the galleries the displayed animals opened their eyes. The snowy owls thrashed against their pins. The elephants stamped their feet. The snow lions and snow leopards arched their backs. On the seventh floor the misery birds opened their eyes, and their wings snapped open to fill their little cold rooms. They lifted each leg and stretched their claws. They spun around upright on their perches. They threw themselves at the doors, and when the doors would not open, they hurled themselves through the glass windows. The glass exploded out over the great courtyard.

In the sword exhibition hall the Neolithic hunters, with their stone ax heads, wiggled their little fingers and opened their eyes. The Teutonic warriors lifted their swords up in the air. A Germanic king, in battle dress, sliced the air in front of him. All of them breathed out one long, frosty breath. The glass display cases shattered.

The crowd in the hall, finger food in hand, forgot to chew.

The large windows split open to reveal Mr. Whittard and the Snow Queen fighting.

They danced, Mr. Whittard and the Snow Queen, they danced across the frosted courtyard; and all around, the snow blew in eddies and drifts; and the wind lifted the Snow Queen's hair so that it seemed to be alive.

"Stop it!" shouted Alice. "Stop it. Leave my father alone." She stamped her diamond-encrusted slipper on the ground.

Ophelia rushed toward her father and the Snow Queen.

"Stay back, Ophelia!" shouted her father.

She saw that the crowd in the sword exhibition hall had broken through the rope cordon to get a better view. They were raising their hands, pointing at the misery birds. The birds were crouched on the rooftops, clinging to the heads of statues with their long gray claws, the icy wind ruffling their feathers and chilling their lonely faces. One by one they let go and swooped down over the courtyard.

"What are they?" screamed Alice as one passed over her.

They circled above the Queen and Mr. Whittard, howling and screeching, and the air was filled with the wind from their monstrous wings.

Ophelia stood in the snow with the magical sword in her hand.

Mr. Whittard and the Snow Queen thrust and parried and spun and lunged until they were inside the great hall. The crowd fell back, slack-mouthed. Ophelia's father lunged forward and, in a striking move, managed to relieve himself of his coat. He parried the Snow Queen's every thrust, and the sounds of their swords rang out in the frozen air.

"What do you want from us?" Mr. Whittard asked.

He sliced the air beside the Snow Queen's face. She spun and lunged at him. He fell as she struck him, a bright red slash across his arm.

The crowd gasped, and the misery birds screeched so loudly that the earth shook.

Mr. Whittard lay where he fell, moaning in pain. Alice ran to his side.

"Shall I finish him off, my beautiful, sad Alice?" said the Snow Queen. She ran the sword over the top of him, not touching him. She stopped and turned slowly.

There was a huge sound, a monstrous sound, a trampling of feet that made the floor tremble. A keening, trumpeting, roaring, growling cacophony. The crowd stood transfixed.

There was Ophelia, standing at the window, sword raised. The Queen's animals stood poised behind her. The elephants and lions and tigers. The snow leopards. The white horses' breaths spiraling in plumes.

The crowd went wild.

Who had ever conceived of such a marvelous show?

"Ophelia," said the Snow Queen.

"Stay back, Ophelia," said her father.

But Ophelia Jane Worthington-Whittard did not stay back. She stepped into the room.

"I am the One Other," said Ophelia. "I am the one that the wizards spoke of."

The Queen held the Great Sorrow up.

"No one can defeat me," said the Snow Queen.

"I can," said Ophelia. "*We* can."

Ophelia's sword leapt at the tiny patch of heat in the Snow Queen's heart. The Snow Queen was too quick, and she parried the thrust. Again they clashed, again they fell apart.

"Ophelia, stop it right now!" shouted Alice. "Can't you see she's dangerous?"

Love, Ophelia's mother whispered. *Love is on your side.*

"Love!" shouted Ophelia. "Love is on our side."

The Snow Queen smirked. Ophelia's sword jerked in her hands. She flew behind it, lunged across the short space until the tip touched the Snow Queen's chest. And the woman fell—simply crumpled—to the floor. She lay there, breathing hard, milk-white breast heaving, a thin trickle of blood on the white satin gown.

"I'm sorry," said Ophelia.

The guards fell to the floor. The birds fell to the ground. The lions, the leopards, the elephants sank down where they stood.

"I'm sorry," said Ophelia again.

She looked in the Snow Queen's eyes, and they were like a girl's eyes, questioning her, sorrowful, but clearing even then, as though she realized.

The lights went out.

There was a vast and deep silence, and then the applause of the crowd.

25

*In which Ophelia must say goodbye
to the Marvelous Boy*

———◆———

Ophelia rushed back across the courtyard. Horatio, she tried. Horace, Henry. Harry, Herbert, Hubert. Hans, Hadrian, Haley. Hallam, Hamish, Hamlet.

She knew none of them was right.

Ignatius, Ivan, Irving. Iago, Ian, Igor. Ike, Imran, Inglebert.

She skated the last few feet until she rested where the Marvelous Boy lay shivering on his side. The snow had stopped falling, and the clouds had broken apart.

"I waited," the boy said. "As long as I could."

He did not ask her if the Snow Queen had been defeated because he knew.

"Beyond the fabled sea there are the mountains," he said. "And beyond those mountains there are the plains, and beyond the plains there are the forest, the river, and the woods, and beyond that there is the town, and I am going to return there."

"I have this for you," said Ophelia. She took the satchel from her shoulder and placed it on the boy. She gave him the biscuit man. "It will give you strength."

"Thank you," he said. The dimple in his cheek showed.

She cried onto his shoulder. "I still don't know your name," she said. "I've only gotten up to *I*."

"The wizards have kept my name so I can return home," the boy said. "And anyway, don't you think we'll meet again?"

"Will we?" asked Ophelia.

She felt his hand move to her hair, a tiny movement, a sigh.

"We have been good friends," said the boy. "We will always be good friends."

He did not say goodbye, but she felt him leave. In the shadows of her closed eyes, she sensed the forest path and saw him there. When she opened her eyes, he was gone. He had simply ceased to be.

Ophelia stood slowly, wiped her eyes, lifted the magical sword at the sky, which was now lightening with stars.

26

In which we say goodbye to
Ophelia Jane Worthington-Whittard

———◆———

After the hospital, where Mr. Whittard had his arm bandaged, they went in a taxi to the hotel. They drove through the streets of the city, where it no longer snowed.

Alice folded all the clothes the museum curator had given her and left them neatly on her bed. She re-dressed herself, the way she had always dressed, in jeans and a T-shirt. She applied blood-red lipstick, which was way too grown-up for her.

The sun was just up. It shone everywhere on the snow and on the glistening white trees and on all the windows. Behind each window there were people waking up to Christmas Day. They would no doubt open their presents, eat, and ice-skate. They would not set a time limit; they would skate into the night, and their cheeks would burn bright, and they would smile. Somewhere a man would take a violin out and begin to play.

At the airport the family's three suitcases were checked and the large, unusually shaped package was checked as well. The unusually shaped package went through the X-ray machine, and security looked very surprised until Ophelia's father produced his card, which read:

MALCOLM WHITTARD

LEADING INTERNATIONAL EXPERT ON SWORDS

They took their seats and rested, waiting for takeoff. Ophelia felt for Alice's hand, and Alice squeezed in return until they were high in the air.

Ophelia looked at her watch. They would be home within a few hours. She went to calculate . . . and stopped.

Be brave, her mother whispered in her ear, and then was gone.

From the airplane window Ophelia could see the city below. All the small and winding gray cobblestone streets, all the shining silver buildings and bridges, the museum, getting smaller and smaller until it was lost.

She caught just a glimpse of the vast and fabled sea before the clouds covered this world. In that tiny moment she fancied she saw blue water, perfect blue water, the whitecaps breaking. Then that view was gone, swallowed up by the whitest clouds she'd ever seen. Ophelia Jane Worthington-Whittard, brave, curious girl, closed her eyes and smiled.

THE END.

ACKNOWLEDGMENTS

Special thanks to my sister, Sonia, for seeing the story and telling me it was worthwhile. Catherine Drayton as well for giving me hope. Erin Clarke for her love of the tale and all her wonderful, passionate work at improving it. Yoko Tanaka for her glorious illustrations. And for my little girl, Alice, who grew up as I was writing it, and who slowly but surely re-opened my eyes to magic.

KAREN FOXLEE worked as a nurse for most of her adult life and also graduated from university with a degree in creative writing. She is the author of *The Midnight Dress* and *The Anatomy of Wings*, which Markus Zusak called "so special that you want to carry it around for months after you've finished, just to stay near it."

Karen Foxlee lives in Gympie, Australia, with her daughter.

5TH-FLOOR GALLERIES

Embroidered Footstools
Life in a Medieval Monastery
Wagons, Spacesuits
Chairs and Cabinets
Mourning Attire
Money and Coins
Famous Letters
Ladies' Fans
Owls

4TH-FLOOR GALLERIES

Culture of the Cossacks
Mesopotamian Mysteries
Customs of Marriage
Napoleonic Wars
The Incas, Egyptian Artifacts
Broken Toys
Very Sharp Medical Devices
Brains in Juice
Superstitions, Dinosaur Hall
A Quaker Kitchen

1ST-FLOOR GALLERIES

The Gallery of Time
Gallery of Old Masters
Taxidermy, Teaspoons
Display of Telephones
Religious Hats
Arcade of Mirrors
Crowns and Tiaras

GROUND FLOOR